LACRIMOSA

RÉGIS JAUFFRET

LACRIMOSA

a novel

Translated from the French by
Vineet Lal

SALAMMBO
PRESS

First published in the United Kingdom in 2011 by

Salammbo Press
39A Belsize Avenue
London NW3 4BN

Originally published in French as *Lacrimosa* by Les Éditions Gallimard, Paris
Copyright © Régis Jauffret and Les Éditions Gallimard, 2008
This English translation copyright © Vineet Lal, 2011

This book is supported by the French Ministry of Foreign Affairs, as part of the Burgess programme run by the Cultural Department of the French Embassy in London (www.frenchbooknews.com).

Liberté · Égalité · Fraternité
RÉPUBLIQUE FRANÇAISE

The translator is grateful for the support of the
British Centre for Literary Translation / Translators Association
translator mentoring programme during his work on this book.

A CIP catalogue record for this book is available from the British Library.

ISBN 9780956808202

Designed and typeset in Sabon by Ateliers Graphiques Ardoisière.
Printed and bound by CPI Group (UK) Ltd, Croydon, CR0 4YY

Dear Charlotte,

You died on a sudden whim from a long illness. Suicide gushed through your brain like an oil spill and you hanged yourself. You had been living in Paris for fourteen years but on 7 June 2007 you took the train to Marseille. As if humans had the memory of an elephant and sometimes returned to dig their grave near the place where, in the past, they'd forced their way out of their mother's womb to set foot in life.

Your parents came to pick you up at Saint-Charles station. You were wearing a blue dress and you switched off your mobile when it rang as your father kissed you. A fifty-something father with a tanned complexion who refused to dye his hair, but was devastated at no longer sparking the slightest flicker of interest in girls' eyes as they walked icily by, blocking out males whose grey hair resembled an old-fashioned flannel beret and dismissing them as dirty old men.

"Maman's made quails with olives."

A dish you had always been haunted by: you probably swallowed your first mouthful when you began sucking your mother's milk. A corny old tune where the olives played the shrill high notes, dancing above a saucepan that bubbled away faithfully like the *basso continuo*.

You complained about the heat.

"The council still hasn't air-conditioned the Old Port."

Neither the Old Port nor the rest of the city. One of those torrid afternoons, when sweat starts to flow from the base of the neck and streams down the crack between your buttocks before petering out God knows where. A sun that foists itself on you like a vulgar lout, even seeming to shine into the dark cellars of old buildings so they blaze like Bedouin tents.

Your father couldn't remember where he'd left the car.

"I think it's on the fifth level down."

He wouldn't listen to your mother, who thought it was parked in the street.

And the deeper the lift plummeted the more you felt it was heading straight for the centre of the earth which, ever since funerals were invented, ought to have been connected to the surface by a wide tube down which corpses could be thrown to roast faster than in a crematorium. The moment you got close to the zone where your father thought he'd left it, the car slipped out of reach. It lugged its carcass from one floor to the next, breaking the law as it crashed through the barrier, until it landed breathlessly at ground level on Rue de l'Étoile, straddling the pavement that runs alongside Saint-Théodore Church.

Your mother let out a sigh. It was precisely where she'd last seen it.

"You never listen to a word I say."

"And I've got a ticket as well."

You told him he always parked any old where.

"In bloody stupid places."

He pulled a face, but it was tinged with good humour.

The car started and so did the heating.

"The air-con's been playing up since yesterday."

Still the smell of leather that made you queasy, even with all four windows open. Memories of being sick during endless journeys to that godforsaken spot in the forest in the Vosges, where you'd go cycling with your sister in the rain to avoid shooting yourselves in the mouth with a hunting gun, bored out of your minds as you were under that veranda, its atmosphere as green as the branches on the surrounding conifers that smashed the windows whenever the wind lifted. Even so, you missed your childhood and those little moments of sadness, fleeting as the bat of an eyelash, with their aftertaste of bubble gum and Coke. But not one bit the black abyss of your teenage years, when you used to picture your skull as a box where you were condemned to live with your feet and fists lashed together, neurons flapping around you like swarms of bats.

"Jérémia's pregnant again, as of last week."

"She's collecting sprogs as though they were cuddly toys."

Your sister lived with a horde of furry animals that still cluttered up her bed. You imagined her husband might sometimes mount a teddy by mistake, astonished that she had become so tiny and hairy, with a virginity as impossible for him to take as it was anachronistic in a woman who'd lost hers at thirteen.

"If it's a girl, she'll have the set."

"She'll keep the less ugly one and sell the other on ebay."

Your father laughed. Your mother looked up and rummaged through her handbag, with the detached expression of a student in philosophy class impulsively slipping a hand under his neighbour's skirt.

"They said on the radio a storm was on its way."

Your mother had turned round to give you this refreshing news which the city's inhabitants had been longing for since the end of the month. Some even dreamt of waterfalls pouring implausibly down the Canebière.

"It's perfect weather for snow."

The joke made her smile and your father burst out laughing, spattering the windscreen with spit that he wiped off with the cloth he used for his glasses. He might even have knocked down a boy in yellow shorts pedalling in front, head tucked into the handlebars, had the kid not decided – for no apparent reason – to sprawl on an old dishwasher abandoned against a lamppost on Boulevard de la Libération. His water-bottle rolled into the road, letting out a squeak as it was squashed by the wheels of the car.

"You still drive like a brute."

"It was just a bottle."

You thought about the grasshoppers you'd chase through the meadows with your sister, ripping off their legs after putting them through a punishing gym class. You promised yourself that when you saw her again you would ask if she still remembered the grey cat you'd found run over by a tractor in a rapeseed field. You'd called it Mewsday and rolled it up in your pullover before placing it in a wheelbarrow, pushing it into a clearing to conduct its funeral that ended with a splash in the pond where you'd thrown its remains as an offering to the pike and carp.

"Mewsday."

"What?"

"You'll piss me off until my dying day."

"Stop it Charlotte."

A father who's still able to laugh while giving you an earful, and a mother with tears in her eyes being careful not to blink or they'll run down her cheeks, hoping you'll be mortified with shame. You think if anyone should be ashamed, it's her. That was the risk she took when she dragged you out of the emptiness where you'd felt so at home. Perhaps, once your father had ejaculated, she'd even contracted the lips of her vulva to keep his penis inside her like a cork, imprisoning his sperm and giving the spermatozoa a chance to make their way deep within her womb, to an ovum frenzied at the thought of uniting, for better or worse, with the first little tadpole to make it there. She'd dragged you along ever since, like a misshapen cannonball that had always refused to roll; and now here she was, presumably allowing herself to sob so you'd feel guilty for being in such a mess when it was she who put you there in the first place. You wished you could formally charge her with childbirth.

However, for several months now you'd been happy. At

least, someone had told you as much one evening on their living room sofa while topping up your glass of Muscat de Frontignan for the third time.

"You're happy, you just don't know it yet."

"I've always known, to be honest."

Your mother is worried about your career. The fashion magazine where you'd been a graphic designer had laid you off at the end of April before going bankrupt half-way through May.

"I'm going to make the most of it and take a year off."

A prospect which did not exactly thrill your parents. They were full of energy, ready to do a full week's work in a day, seventeen million hours a year – even when they were dead if, in the afterlife, there happened to be a business prepared to employ them despite their freshly-dug-up appearance.

"Your father and I don't waste our time."

There was no question of them frittering away rare moments of relaxation by standing and staring. At fifty-five time becomes precious and throwing it down the drain amounts to throwing yourself down there as well. Rather than squandering it from day to day like pocket money, it can be stashed away in gilt-edged investments that offer a high return in well-being and pleasure of all kinds. Even if sport is tiring and exasperating, it allows the brain to generate stimulating endorphins, helping one appreciate trips to Italy, Quebec and Guatemala, and the fire in the hearth when it's cold enough to enjoy toasting oneself in front of the flames and forgetting about the central heating whose boiler, in any case, has aged so prematurely it's starting to belch.

Your mother is on a roll now.

"Why, I even emailed Maya Coufin this morning to say how much I'm in love with life."

"At your age, you really ought to try out those coffins they've got on offer at the hypermarket so you get used to lying in a box."

"We could also go hearse racing."

Your father can already picture himself skidding along in pole position on a snowy Alpine road inside a hearse decked out in the colours of Olympique de Marseille who'd surely agree to sponsor him seeing he was a junior player at the Stade Vélodrome when he was nine. He chortles so much he bangs his head on the steering wheel, while your mother ferrets gloomily through the glove compartment as if hoping to find a revolver to shoot the pair of you.

"You've gone past Rue Daumier."

A slightly dodgy reverse to Rue Daumier; then the gate closes behind the car. Your father grabs your red canvas bag, throwing it down in the hall like some insufferable baby ditched at the very last minute before one's reduced to strangling it to make it stop howling like a broken speaker.

"And now, champagne."

"No, we'll wait for Jérémia."

"We'll open another when she's here."

Your father is already in the kitchen, diving into the fridge.

You stretch out on the chaise longue. A pretentious piece of furniture you've always borne a grudge against. You dig your heels into the fabric to widen the gash you managed to create last winter, after a war of attrition that ended in you taking some aspirin to ease your aching Achilles tendons.

You're thinking of nothing else; you're unaware of the imminent ambush, the preparations for battle being made deep inside you, the gathering troops, the bombers laden with deadly cargo, the submarines on manoeuvre peeping through the surface of your consciousness with periscopes. You don't see that black dot on the horizon, mistaking it for a speck of dirt. You tell yourself you're no longer living in the dark. But rather in the clear light of dawn, with a sun that occasionally shows itself long enough to make you believe it's rising.

You've heard the cork popping. The glass teeters before your eyes in a hand that's veined and freckled. You offer your lips and your father tilts the glass. You sit bolt upright again when your mother starts yelling at you to stop being so childish. She has a knife in her hand.

"You look like an executioner's wife."

"I'm hulling the strawberries."

You retreat to the first floor. The toilet lid is awash with colour: it used to be so very black, and now it's a red you find obscene. But there's still the same solitary nail stuck in the door. You've always wondered whether the game actually consisted of throwing your knickers at it, scoring a point whenever you succeeded in hooking them on like a ring. The chain on the flush must date back to when bogs were invented, its wooden handle so worn in the middle that it's now as bulbous as a penis.

You pass your room. The window is open. The chest of drawers gapes at you, the drawers sticking their tongues out. They probably think you're going to make the effort to fill them with your belongings instead of leaving your stuff in the bag and taking things out as you go along, like tissues from a box.

"I've made your bed."

Your mother is right behind you. She offers you a bathrobe and a towel. Her voice has aged since your last visit; you picture her vocal cords streaked with little wrinkles similar to the ones that sit like a moustache above her lips. In thirty or forty years from now it'll be your duty to bury her, and your father too. You'll certainly have to be up at first light for that. They always rush through funerals early in the morning so the undertakers can spend the afternoon at the beach.

"I've given the drawers a bit of a wash."

"You could have given the ceiling a quick shower too."

"They should be dry by now."

She crouches down to feel them and you want to give her a kick. So she'll lose her balance, shrinking enough to take up no more room than a doll in the bottom drawer. A nicely tidied-away mother for you to carry back to Paris like a mascot under your T-shirt. A compressed mother,

15

like a brand-new sponge who only needs soaking in water every evening to swell up and hold you in her arms. Her hugs will be slightly damp, of course.

"Jérémia just called."

"Someone must have taught her to use the phone."

"She's left Pindo with Branton's parents."

Pindo, a name fit for a turkey: your sister could always cook her little one for Christmas if the poulterers went on strike. And Branton, bearded and almost bald, a wheeler and dealer in humanitarian affairs. A pitiful individual who in your opinion liked others more than himself, and was probably imagining Jérémia as a ragged old tramp when he paid homage to her.

Your mother was silent and then blurted out a sentence. As though she wanted to be rid of it.

"Your father seems happy, but he's sad."

"You ought to have his prostate taken out."

"I think he's worried about Pindo."

She cried. Such a cute child, but so ugly. Sweet and gentle, but with a look of despair about him, even at the age of one. A baby whose future was off-limits, his entire life wasted. As if he were a dustbin overflowing with all the failures, cowardice, kowtowing and nights of sordid liaisons, like the guilty onanism of the mystics, that made up his existence – one that was useless to others and harmful to himself. His story paced backwards and forwards like a sentry. It lay in wait. The screenplay for his life could already be read in his face and staring too long at his eyes revealed every scene in storyboard form. When filming was over, Pindo might (at the very most) enjoy the privilege of becoming a drop in the ocean of statistics concerning the mortality rate of Westerners born in February 2006.

"Me too, I'm worried sick."

Your mother's tears were absorbed by the straps of your blue dress. A few, though, dripped onto your bare shoulder where they triggered off tiny spots of irritation. As though you were allergic to her grief.

You had never run your hand through her hair. You'd never felt her head with your fingers. You were doing it for the first time. You might even have consoled her, had she continued to remain silent. Had you not realised that now she was talking to you about yourself. You tensed up, resisting, so as not to hear her words. You thought you'd succeed in dodging them. Like bullets.

You shouted.

"Shut up, I'm not listening."

She said nothing more. You should have left the room. Because, shattering the silence, her words – which you'd managed not to hear until then, and which seemed to have fizzled out – began to resonate once more, piercing, turning into a howl, and you pushed her away, covering your ears like someone under bombardment.

Yet whenever she'd insisted that you be happy, her tone had been so gentle. She thought children who were miserable ended up dragging their parents through the mud.

"Happiness is a matter of willpower."

You'd have showered her with abuse. But she wouldn't

have understood. In fact she had already fallen silent, perhaps for several minutes. You'd have tried explaining in vain that her injunctions sometimes wandered far and wide before reaching you, like a long-distance radio signal.

You come downstairs. Reality seems to be crumbling in front of you. It's in freefall, fatal freefall. Life no longer looks anything like itself; perhaps you're already hanging upstairs. Hair continues to grow after you die, and you wonder whether the brain, for its part, carries on thinking. You tell yourself it doesn't. But it seems likely.

You find your father again on the ground floor. You recognise him, but something about him is more intense. He's fooling around with the remote, grinning and grimacing at the faces that appear and disappear, glowing like reflections on the screen of the old cathode ray television – constructed long ago by Japanese workers in a factory relocated to a developing country in 1999.

"Pindo's lucky."

Your father hangs his head, as if you'd been talking about a crow that would wake him up three times a night for a year by pecking at his eyes.

"Maman's grieving for him while he's still alive."

"She might as well."

He begins to laugh, no doubt imagining his grandson all togged up in a desperate employee's brown uniform, perpetually stalked by some diabolical, amputated foot that's constantly taking a run at his pathetic bottom to give it a sound kicking, like the gob of an ashtray stained by thousands of cigarettes stubbed out around its rim.

"Someone could really do with a good abortion."

"Perhaps he'll be lucky enough to get strangled by a maniac."

"Those people have far too much taste to relieve distressed families of their pain."

You think your father is being too negative. You're convinced that, in the name of equal opportunities, an open-minded paedophile would agree to wring Pindo's neck with as much venom as he'd spew on a brilliant child destined for fame and fortune.

"And Jérémia'll be here soon."

"She's not bringing Pindo."

"I don't like your sister."

Loving both daughters at the same time was like cheating on one with the other. A father must choose between his children; he can no more love them all than decide to sleep with every woman in creation.

"That wouldn't be fair."

Your mother appears. She's crept downstairs, shoes in hand. She pours herself a glass, sniffing the layer of bubbles fizzing on the surface. She empties it, gargles and swallows the warm champagne, putting her hand up to her Adam's apple.

"My throat was dry."

"Pindo must have made you thirsty."

"That child will drive me mad."

Her chin has grown all of a sudden. Her jaw now sticks out as though she's gone crazy. She kicks the little side table. The peanuts jump around in their dish and the bottle nods in agreement.

You go back to the chaise longue, having resolved to work at it with your heels until all its stuffing spills out like foam. It's still sunny in the garden but for you it feels like darkness has fallen. An opaque night, obscuring the stars. So dark that no electric light can puncture it. It has made endless little fissures from your thoughts, crevices into which you'll disappear forever. You're stretched out on the chaise longue, just as you will be on the zinc table the following day when the coroner examines the marks on your neck, muttering absent-mindedly into his voice recorder.

"Death by strangulation."

He almost lit up a cigarette, but looking at the flame from his lighter he remembered he'd been sent a memorandum the day before to the effect that smoking was no longer permitted anywhere in the forensics laboratory.

"Even in the dissecting room."

As if corpses occasionally woke up and died again on the spot, having suddenly contracted bronchial cancer. As if the deceased were returned to their families with their hair smelling unbearably of nicotine or with bits of ash stuck to their livers.

"No autopsy. Put her back in the fridge."

You were plunged into the light once more on hearing your sister and her husband, their voices all jumbled together as they rose through the air in the room, like a pair of besotted grass snakes transfixed by a snake charmer's flute on Place Jamaa Lafna.

"Pindo smiled at us when we left him with Branton's mother."

So the little one had become hypocritical enough to show his teeth, whereas in fact he was so distressed he was close to chewing off the insides of his cheeks and swallowing them, turning his face into a three-dimensional reflection of his internal misery.

Your mother was scowling in a corner by the fireplace; your father lay slumped on the sofa, mechanically punching the cushions and bitterly burping up all the champagne he'd drunk.

"You've grown even taller."

"So has Pindo."

In any case, you found it increasingly ridiculous that your sister carried on growing like this despite being twenty-two. While she'd been a midget as a teenager, she was now taller than the lightshade and would soon be able to repaint the ceilings of Notre-Dame-de-la-Garde with her tongue without needing to perch on a stepladder.

As for Branton, he looked like a dwarf. A dwarf who grew smaller and smaller each time his humanitarian rage diminished him in his own eyes when he compared the pinprick of his life to the millions of tonnes of Earthlings who by 2150 would have died from starvation, pollution or even hypothermia, when the erratic climate sent forth a deluge of rain mixed with hail after three decades of heatwaves. The more he appeared to shrink, the more your sister seemed to assume the proportions of a bell-tower.

Your father signalled to the young couple that he intended going to bed early that evening. He took off his

watch and pressed it against Branton's nose, which sank into his face like a nail.

"It's gone ten past seven."

"Pindo must be eating his baby food."

"Get some bread and ham, and eat them outside."

"Pindo adores ham."

Your father took a hundred euro note from his jacket pocket.

"This is for you, if you bugger off and take your Branton too."

"I think Pindo will grow to love money when he's bigger, the other day he was sucking on a coin."

Your mother swallowed Jérémia's head whole like an oyster.

You went up to your room, and at the bottom of your bag you found a scarf. They said afterwards this was what you'd used to hang yourself.

"A very strong scarf, then."

The detective was amazed by your determination. To have made a noose, slipped your head through and attached the other end firmly to the window handle.

"Bracing herself, in a way."

Launching yourself, like pulling the trigger, deciding to fire. The vertebrae were snapped cleanly apart.

"Her mother found her."

Your body in her arms. The scarf now starting to tear, as if it suddenly realised it ought to have done so before. Your body doubled over, a big dead foetus, still warm, that she'll start to carry once more. When their daughters die, women's bellies swell up again for the rest of their lives. They are much heavier than the first time around.

My poor darling,

Nothingness has been telling emptiness some very odd
things indeed. Word is they recently exchanged a juicy bit
of gossip where I was the butt of the joke. Some piece of
idle chit-chat about me and my family, which might lead us
to think we're in one of your demeaning stories where you
love to mock the poor people who've fallen prey to your
twisted mind. Can shame never stifle your imagination?
Will you always prefer extravagance to people?

It also seems you're now addressing me in the tone you'd
use for a passer-by. Have I become so distant? And what
gives you the right to name me after a pudding? As though
it wasn't enough that when I was born my parents
lumbered me with the name of a beast of burden? Of
course, I can't be sure about anything; we only get rumours
and tittle-tattle here, and we do wonder what's blowing
them around, given how stagnant and thin the air is. To be
frank, now that I haven't any air at all, I'm inclined to think
my lungs invented it every time I took a breath.

Do you think it's easy here, reading letters from weirdos to girls who've tossed their lives and caution to the wind, like a pair of jeans worn to shreds, just to be given a gorgeous made-to-measure wooden dress? Do you think it's like being in a hotel, with a writing desk under a picture of a mountain lake framed in exotic wood, letterheaded paper and room service for whenever we're dehydrated by the central heating and get the urge to drink a cup of Earl Grey tea? You might as well ring me while you're at it! Perhaps you'd like my email into the bargain? Something along the lines of nothingnesscharlotte@deathifyoufeellikeit?

And another thing: there aren't many shopping arcades at the bottom of a hole. They're closed night and day, and the staff are on strike the rest of the time. So there's no chance of going to buy a notepad, a ballpoint and a clementine-scented rubber. As for the postmen – do you think they're dedicated enough to unscrew the coffins so letters from the living can get to their addressees? I suppose you also believe that when someone has nothing left in their eye-sockets, the graveyard caretaker is generous enough to scurry over and lend them his glasses?

Death doesn't have any windows, you know; going jogging is always an option to give our skeletons a golden glow. No candles either, or electricity, because decomposition produces highly flammable gases and the smallest flame, or the slightest spark, could make our rickety boxes blow up like booby-trapped cars.

Seeing as I've only got tiny worms where my optic nerve should be, how do you expect me to consult your pile of prattle without any light? You prattle-snake, always kipping on your keyboard, chattering, nattering with your liquid crystals that arouse you like pussies!

Poor darling, poor old owl, writing all night like a messy-haired clerk. Go to bed instead of staying up. Get into the habit of waking early. Of going for walks in the forest. Of drinking water. Of giving up Nicot's weed. At your age you should know that happy people live like animals. Death is no laughing matter: try living a few more years. Two or three decades, or you could even summon up the courage to get past June 2055. By then there will be more centenarians than babies. Seize the day.

One more thing. Before closing this letter, I want you to imagine that my feelings for you disappeared along with my final thoughts. When people are a bit under the weather, it's comforting to think someone loved them once.

Dear Charlotte,

Your mother had given Jérémia her head back: it emerged from her gaping mouth as if she were laying a big hairy egg. Then she heard you falling and dying upstairs, and in a state of general indifference went off to find you.

Your sister complained the gastric juices had left her short-sighted. Branton promised to fish her out a pair of contact lenses at Third World Optometry where he'd been appointed sales director the year before, when Eardrums Without Borders had fired him following a period of sick leave brought on by earache.

"I'll manage with a fuzzy view of Pindo meanwhile."

Your father's phone rang.

"Hello."

Your mother broke the news of your little prank using the mobile that had tumbled from the pocket of your blue dress. In the weeks that followed the handset would ring seventeen times before the battery was finally drained of its remaining charge. For a fortnight people continued to leave the occasional message on your voicemail. On the second-last Thursday in June, Branton came up with the idea of terminating your contract and donating your handset to

Fone-Aid. It was to finish up in the hands of a starving mother, who hadn't as yet been driven crazy enough by malarial fever to mistake it for a bar of chocolate and give it to her offspring to eat; they were thin and pot-bellied, and squatted like old people beneath a rusty metal Pepsi-Cola hoarding that had functioned as a shelter ever since a tropical storm had carried it to their village, all battered and stinking of rotting human flesh.

Your father hung up. His hair looked darker because his face had gone as white as yoghurt.

"Charlotte's dead."

"I'll always be scared of Pindo falling into water when he's out on his bike."

Your father went upstairs on legs that carried him like two Sherpas. You were lying in your mother's arms. Like a Madonna with Child, or a Pietà, but instead of a crucified man there was just a young woman who'd hanged herself.

She held the mobile clenched in her hand as though expecting the sound of its ringing to resurrect your flesh. Your father paralysed in the doorway, the Sherpas refusing to advance any further. He was crying dry tears that left little burn marks down his pale cheeks.

Jérémia had opened the fridge door. She peered intently at the food while Branton stared at the quails and pecked at the olives set in the thick sauce. Through the open window it was clear that daylight hadn't quite given up yet. A thin white cloud, shaped like a one-armed man, kissed the left-hand edge of the frame. The bells of Saint-Giniez Church had fallen silent, unable to strike eight o'clock because the belfry was being repaired. A child was crying on the first floor of the building next door and a woman was busy clattering some plates around.

"I've always thought Pindo wouldn't like quails with olives."

Branton put the dish in the microwave. Jérémia took a baguette from the linen bread bag. She cut it using a knife with serrations so fine it tended to slip on the crust. They didn't hear the silence that had fallen over the bedroom upstairs, where the heat couldn't prevent it from coating your parents like a layer of frost. Upstairs, where nothing would happen any more because you'd gone off, leaving behind your body and your travel bag. Notes and chords evaporate once they've been played, even if the piano itself continues to gleam with all the blackness of its lacquer and the whiteness of its keys. Your mother would have loved to vanish along with you. In a puff.

"What a strange idea."

Jérémia was dumbfounded.

"What a strange idea, Charlotte, you being dead."

"Death's not something you can export."

Branton felt people were already exporting way too much to under-developed countries: too much industrial waste, too many wars and violent attacks. Their populations inherited our rubbish without enjoying any of the benefits. We couldn't ask each person to die several times over into the bargain; we might as well insist they gave birth to themselves on our behalf too, sending us disinfected planeloads of pre-weaned babies to save us the hassle of delivering them ourselves. Filtering our lives for us, suffering every ounce of the world's pain, and leaving us nothing more than a legacy of carefree abandon, so the only bit of life we'd be left with was the living. As if birth and death accounted for our most cumbersome bits of baggage and we'd refused to lug them around any longer.

"If someone were to die Pindo's death for him, he'd be shot of it forever."

"There's nothing to suggest we'll ever have the necessary know-how."

"Death's a worry for any mother."

"Death's ecological, we get recycled."

"I demand that Pindo live forever."

The microwave pinged; the quails were hot.

Branton put the dish on the table. Jérémia took two fondue forks out of a drawer. Each of them speared one of the little beasts and they patted each other contentedly with every mouthful. The very act of eating, they felt, distinguished them from their faraway corpse that would now eat so little.

"Charlotte should have had her dinner."

"She chose to die on an empty stomach."

"When she was little, she used to spit her calves' liver out on the floor."

But Branton said she'd wanted to show her support for all those dying of hunger with every second that ticked by.

"In other words, never eating a thing."

"She should at least have tasted the sauce out of respect for Maman."

Branton wrapped a quail and three olives in a piece of foil. Then he slipped the package into a plastic bag. He stuffed the whole thing into the deep side pocket of his baggy salmon-coloured cotton trousers.

"I'll send her share to the Congo."

"It'll go off on the boat."

"That's true."

He threw the packet away. Jérémia opened the fridge door again.

"There's some strawberries in wine."

They ate them with both hands, collecting the juice in their palms and pouring it as best they could into their mouths. When they'd emptied the bowl their faces were all red and sticky, as though they'd just murdered one of their nearest and dearest. They cleaned themselves, after a fashion.

Jérémia put the coffee maker on.

"I hope the parents are coming down for coffee."

"Maybe we should phone a doctor."

"I'll call Dr Dupré."

Jérémia went upstairs. Night was falling and the onshore breeze was saving its breath to create a few late-evening waves. The city was still inhaling the saturated air that had left it gasping all day like a feverish patient. And yet your mother now held in her arms a corpse as cold as the marble on the still-gaping chest of drawers.

Jérémia threw herself at you. She gave you a slap.

"Charlotte, you've been a bloody pain in the arse."

She was thinking about the last Christmas dinner. That sentence you'd come out with, so blatantly out of place.

"I often committed suicide when I was younger, but I haven't done it for ages."

This was followed by a laugh, and everyone else had to laugh too so as not to leave you feeling alone. To stop you realising just how alone you were, lost inside yourself, on a little part of yourself, detached from yourself, floating within yourself, where you were poking fun at yourself, as if you were someone else, not you.

"You're a bloody pain in the arse."

You father grabs hold of her. He gives her a kick; your mother steps in to receive it instead before he succeeds in immobilising Jérémia on the floor. Your sister is suddenly calm, almost limp. Your father moves backwards to the bed and drops down. When she gets up again, he stares at her long and hard.

"You're right, she's a pain in the arse."

It looked like he was about to start sobbing.

"Dr Dupré said he'd be here by eleven."

And, having made this announcement, Jérémia went back downstairs. Leaving your parents motionless again, the skeleton embedded in their flesh like a foot in a tight-fitting shoe.

Your corpse was now as stiff as a board. Your sister's

hand was already beginning to swell up. If she'd slapped you a second time she would have had nothing but a fleshy glove left at the end of her arm, a mitten filled with fragments of carpals, metacarpals and shattered phalanges.

There was a tap on the little window in the front door.

"Hello, doctor."

"Let's see what's wrong with her now."

They had got into the habit of summoning Dr Dupré for the slightest cough, and each time Charlotte had felt even vaguely depressed in the past he'd been sent for as a matter of some urgency. He'd long ago come to terms with having to abandon consultations straightaway: putting aside his plate of steak and French beans or jumping out of bed at three in the morning to get to Rue Daumier while still half-asleep, but nevertheless attempting to run all the way there from his home in Rue Paradis as it was clearly too near to justify taking the car.

"I told you on the phone she was dead."

"Easy for you to say."

"She's hanged herself."

"She's always hanging herself, the first time she was barely eleven."

Jérémia followed the doctor. He laid his briefcase on the coffee table and threw his bottom violently down onto the sofa.

"Tell her to get here quickly."

"She's not the least bit alive."

"She'll hear me."

Dr Dupré leapt to his feet and, launching himself off the sofa springs as effortlessly as if they were a trampoline, promptly appeared bang in the middle of your bedroom. He'd forgotten his briefcase downstairs. Jérémia had only just got to the third step on the staircase when he ordered her to bring it to him in a high-pitched voice that showed his irritation. He greeted your parents, still rooted to the spot, by sketching a sort of comma in mid-air with his pointed nose that seemed as sharp as a pen nib.

"And what's more, she's pissed herself."

Men ejaculate when they hang themselves. As a woman you had to settle for leaving a dribble of urine on the floor, and abandon all hope of seeing a mandrake growing out of the tiles at dawn.

"And about time too!"

Gasping for breath, Jérémia held out his briefcase. She found her parents exactly as she'd left them shortly before, lying in dry dock on the floor and on the bed, as though waiting to be repainted before being floated again.

"I'm going to give her an adrenaline injection."

In his view this remedy was the ultimate weapon in the battle against sloppiness, laziness and apathy. He sucked up the contents of a yellowish phial into a syringe as fine as a dropper. He approached this mother now conjoined like a twin to her dead daughter. She saw him coming, her face sullen and teeth clenched in exasperation. He rubbed your arm with a piece of cotton wool soaked in spirit. He drove the needle in abruptly. The liquid refused to penetrate the muscle. It trickled away haphazardly between two beauty spots on your milky-white skin. He shook you and your mother hugged you even tighter. She was trying to shield you from this madman, whereas a moment earlier she'd perhaps still believed in his grotesque little schemes. As if, ill-equipped to kill, this sort of absurdity could occasionally bring someone back to life.

"Actually, what this scatterbrain really needs is to carry on being dead."

He launched the syringe like a dart. It landed in the skirting board.

"All I can do is ask for her to be committed."

It would take a psychiatrist energetic enough to make her see sense through shock therapy.

"I don't give a damn whether she loves being alive or not, she'll drink the elixir of life down to the last drop."

Your father got up. As cool and detached as a robot, he pushed Dr Dupré out of the room; the doctor began sliding on the soles of his new moccasins with all the grace of a skier on a hard-packed snow slope. On reaching the stairs, he fell flat on his back and waited until he'd reached the ground floor before assuming an upright position. Feeling a bump hatching out on his forehead, he swerved off to the living room to splash himself with water from the champagne bucket. The ice had melted and the water had warmed up. His next stop was the kitchen where he applied the ice cube tray to his skull.

He eventually judged he'd slowed down the growth of his bump as much as he could.

"I have no wish to look like a hammerhead shark."

He picked up the half-full bottle of wine used to prepare the strawberries, taking several swigs to settle his frayed nerves and give him the strength to continue drinking the elixir of life for a few more years.

Upstairs, it felt as though the world was about to slip from the Frost Era into the Ice Age. Your father had become fossilised in the bedroom doorway. He was still pushing the doctor with his hands. Even though Dr Dupré had become invisible and intangible, and wasn't even there any more. Your mother had wrapped herself around you like the shell covering an egg. Or maybe she'd sat on you like a brooding hen in the hope of seeing you hatch and hearing you chirp like a chick, wailing like a baby of twenty-four who, having briefly flirted with death, has to learn to walk all over again.

She'd gladly have raised you a second time, and many more besides, had you played that trick of dying and coming back to life on her one more time. She would have loved to joke with you about this short-term death. You'd both have chuckled as you talked about a scarf now barely fit to end its days in a cupboard, only being dragged out for a game of blind man's buff. A slightly morbid version, the kind people must have played in the Middle Ages during the *danses macabres* on Mardi Gras. But in truth, your frozen corpse had infected the room which was now as cold as a mortuary.

"That's all I needed, going out on call and not getting paid."

Dr Dupré had always hated this sort of senseless extravagance. He demanded payment for every visit, no matter how brief. Even his cousin Canasta, a stupid old woman whose poverty was matched only by her allergy to the peas she periodically binged on to challenge her metabolism, had to cough up the cash every time the foul-tempered doctor wrote her a prescription in red ink for anti-histamines – signalling to the chemist that this patient had to be kicked out swiftly and kept under surveillance.

"And anyway, after eight it counts as a night call."

He thought he also remembered that, two years earlier, he'd met you in the street when you had a cold and suggested you take some aspirin without this costing you so much as a penny. He wouldn't have known exactly what to charge for this slightly off-the-cuff advice. And that evening your father had proved so ill-tempered that, had he dared ask for the slightest remuneration, the doctor might have received a clip round the ear rather than one of those pretty cheques decorated with an engraving of the Vallon des Auffes that he'd so often been treated to. To avoid such disappointment he decided to pay himself in kind.

He seized hold of the tartan shopping trolley parked in front of him next to the broom cupboard, and set about filling it with bars of chocolate and tartlets (the ones in those cute boxes with kittens) as well as a brand-new jar of honey he promised himself as a delightful treat for Sunday breakfast.

"I'll take some sardines in oil, artichoke hearts and foie gras as well."

The trolley wasn't even half full. He finished off his

shopping spree with an old orange whisk that had been languishing on a shelf since the late eighties in its original packaging and two Murano glass knick-knacks portraying a lamb with his flute-playing shepherd. Your parents had been given them as an engagement present by a prankster of a friend and treasured them so much they'd stashed them away at the back of a drawer in the hall table.

But for the tinkling of a tiny bell connected to his innate sense of integrity, reminding him that greed was merely younger sister to the voracity of thieves, the doctor would even have helped himself to an old golden fob watch which lay idling, along with some foreign coins, at the bottom of a box that had started its career full of sugared almonds at a christening.

The doctor made his way back up Rue Daumier, pushing his load ahead of him like a night owl who's just been shopping at the 24-hour grocery store to prepare a fine supper for his lover; she's sitting there starving with an empty plate, hammering it with the tips of her red-varnished nails spangled with mica. A stone's throw from his block he exchanged a few words with Mme Taboulet, a neighbour disfigured by the faces she'd got into the habit of making in the bathroom mirror to take her mind off losing her husband.

"I'm getting married again."

"Not to me, Mme Taboulet, for I am taken."

"You don't have to marry another person. Nowadays you can get unipolar couples."

"You could also turn yourself into a snail."

"What a thing to say, Dr Dupré."

She made a face at him. It was her way of wishing him goodnight.

"I shall sleep well, Mme Taboulet. It's exhausting taking care of the dead."

The doctor had always been afraid of lifts, suspecting their cabins devoured their passengers as rapaciously as fly-eating carnivorous plants. He climbed the stairs carrying the shopping trolley on his back, like a Father Christmas who'd apparently got both the season and his choice of outfit badly wrong. His briefcase, the handle held tightly between his teeth, hovered in front of him like a rectangular black leather beard full of medical equipment, phials and pills. He wouldn't have been able to get his keys from his pocket without setting down his load; but, thank heavens, the door had been converted to voice recognition at the turn of the millennium, and opened without a word being spoken when it heard him straining with exhaustion on the fourth-floor landing.

"You ought to be in bed, Mazda."

"Grr."

Dr Dupré co-habited with a female panda he had seduced in central China during a study tour on Mandarin nasal therapy, organised by a safety pin manufacturer who intended to go into alternative medicine. No matter how many private lessons he'd tried organising with a retired schoolmistress on Place Thiars, the stubborn creature had never made any effort to learn French. She always communicated in a very rudimentary Chinese, the kind peasant farmers in the Yichang region would have used in the age of the brontosaurs – a time when this city was still no more than a hamlet of caves, where people shivered all winter long given no-one had as yet thought of inventing fire.

"Come on Mazda, it's time for bed."

"Grr."

His partner followed him into the bedroom. The couple planted themselves in front of the rose-pink earthenware basin, set into a wall covered in grey-blue hessian and next to a Provençal wardrobe whose wood Mazda had scratched with her claws as she despised country-style furniture. Each of them took a toothbrush, one between his fingers and the other between her paws, and complied in unison with the laws of oral hygiene. Then they lay down in a large bed with springs that had buckled under the panda's weight. Because this was one of those giant pandas that are as heavy as a buffalo and wiggle their hindquarters up and down in their sleep to scare off fleas. They dozed off, but only after Mazda had smashed the bedside lamp to bits with one whack of her snout.

Yet Dr Dupré didn't just have the little bell of integrity tinkling in his ear: at the centre of his brain was a gong of crazy ideas that would reverberate each time a problem was gnawing away at him. That night, in the middle of Episode 1070 of a long dream sequence that had begun three years earlier – and in which he was a travelling monk in the mid-14th century, wandering high and low to treat the bubonic plague – the gong suddenly sounded in his head, shattering his dream and making his skull vibrate until the bone cracked.

"Grr."

Mazda was hardly ecstatic about him leaping out of bed so abruptly and putting on the light to slip hurriedly into his clothes as though he had to get to the nuclear shelter on Rue du Commandant-Rolland to shield himself from radiation caused by a nuclear missile, fired accidentally by a submariner with a veiny nose (thanks to his fondness for plonk) and targeted at the municipal swimming pool in Plan-de-Cuques which any Puss-in-Seven-League-Boots could reach from Rue Paradis in a single stride.

"Grr."

"Go back to sleep, Mazda, I'll cut up a mango for your breakfast."

Before leaving, Dr Dupré turned off the power to make sure not a single lamp, not one fluorescent tube would be so bold as to light up while he was away and disturb his other half as she slept. He'd forgotten that the *livarot* cheese would melt in the fridge and the whiting bought that very morning from Baptiste Triton, the young fishmonger on Place Delibes, would end up with its skin drained of all colour and its flesh taking on the vile smell of ammonia.

"Gaston Kiwi."

. The doctor repeated the name aloud as he went down

43

Boulevard Périer. He was the very person he'd thought of when the gong had made his dream explode.

"Gaston Kiwi."

A kind of clever philosopher who had always viewed metaphysics as a bag of tricks to be used just as one pleased for stitching together lives falling apart at the seams, or doubling one's time to ease a packed schedule.

Sir Kiwi never slept at night, considering darkness the work of the devil and liable to reduce people to ashes if they didn't scare it away every hour by waving a lantern on the roof, as if winking at the stars. When the doctor arrived at Impasse Harmonide, Kiwi was, as it happened, perched on the tiled roof of his cottage, and with a sweeping gesture seemed to be offering his lamp to the moon to graze on.

"Gaston, old friend."

"Hippocampus, how marvellous."

Gaston alone knew his bizarre first name (with its scent of the sea and hint of a horse) and even his closest friends called him Édouard. He performed a standing jump into the arms of the doctor. The lantern, unfortunately, landed smack on Dr Dupré's parietal bone and barely a second later his head had been transformed into a ball of fire. Gaston tried to put it out by reeling off a torrent of Thomist speculations on the Fundamental Causes of the Flood. But with the smell of grilled chops beginning to drift through the air, he decided to go and fetch the fire extinguisher that stood guard in its red uniform in his oratory, ready to smother the flames of the Holy Spirit in case of an emergency. When he had finished spraying him down, the doctor's head looked like a snowman waiting for someone to stick a carrot in the very middle of his face.

"Come in and give your face a wash, Hippocampus."

The doctor's features re-emerged once cleansed with warm water. The blisters did nothing to make him more attractive but they did add a certain reddish quality to skin that was normally as pale and smooth as icing.

"Kiwi, I've a dead woman on my hands."

"Metaphysics is crazy about this stuff."

"We need to get her out of this."

Kiwi was leaning out of the window, keeping a close eye on the moon. In a gesture of solidarity and with his heart filled with hope, the doctor stared at it too, his little eyes hovering above his nose like pips in a slice of watermelon. But suddenly, with a hefty thrust of his back, Kiwi teleported himself and re-appeared right in front of the trapdoor that led to the basement of his tiny hermit-like dwelling, a move that sent his friend rolling head over heels across the lino.

"Quick, Hippocampus, the bikes."

For several years now, some ancient bikes had been hanging on the cellar's saltpetred walls like mutineers in the hold of the *Bounty*. The two friends brought them back up to the surface, panting under the weight of their rust. Kiwi re-inflated their tyres with a puff of divine breath he just happened to have bottled a week earlier in the crypt of Saint-Victor Abbey, while the doctor dusted off their saddles with the back of his sleeve. And then they were off on their steeds, like ramshackle knights embarking on a quest for an unlikely Grail.

The bikes creaked and weren't in the least happy about having to bear the men's weight during the tough climb up Rue Fargès. As he mercilessly cranked away on the pedals Gaston Kiwi talked to the doctor, trying to explain a theory so woolly he began coughing like a patient in the last stages of bronchial cancer.

"If the house recedes, the earth will have to recede as well."

They arrived in Rue Daumier. Kiwi continued to philosophise without pausing for breath.

"A metaphysician sometimes has a duty to pooh-pooh the laws of universal gravitation."

The exhausted bikes flopped down on the pavement.

"You really are a pair of lazy so-and-sos."

Taking aim at the pot-bellied chains, Kiwi gave them a thumping whack with one of his knock-knees. The rock-solid blow made them sit upright at once, whining plaintively like slaves who've been given a dressing-down.

"Mount!"

Our two heroes got back in the saddle. The road ahead was clear because the moment you breathed your last the gate to your house sprang wide open, like a tombstone gaping at the city.

The tyres, almost flat despite the blast of air Kiwi had given them before leaving, were racked with pain as they confronted the pebbles in the garden.

"Let's go for it, Hippocampus, we've got to hit this head-on."

They charged towards the façade at a snail's pace. And, at the very last moment, the terrified bikes refused to confront the obstacle that was only vaguely lit up by the distant halo of a lamppost, set back under one of the plane trees in the street. Rearing up, the contraptions threw their riders to the ground and fled immediately for fear of reprisals. It transpired later they'd been hobbling around Marseille and reliable witnesses had seen them loitering on the Corniche. They had jumped over the parapet, plunged into the sea and perished.

"We'll do without those cowards."

The partners in crime picked themselves up, massaging backsides that ached like hell.

"Let's take a run at it, Hippocampus."

Kiwi led the doctor to Avenue du Prado.

"Catch your breath, Hippocampus."

They ran back up the street, their running so inept it looked like they were limping. They finally crashed feebly into the house. Which, alas, did not budge an inch.

"This building is stubborn."

Lying flat on his belly on the gravel, exasperated and mad with rage, Kiwi beat erratically at the door with his fists. But this time the house made an unexpected gesture of goodwill – so proving, dear Charlotte, that it had a soft spot for you, that it too had loved you. It remembered the baby that cried deep within its bowels, the child who smashed one of its shutters in a fit of anger one day with a pétanque ball, the girl who secretly wept and made love on the broken-legged old sofa that had been banished to the attic as punishment for two or three generations.

"Gravitation, Hippocampus."

It admitted defeat. The house lowered its head and, with all its strength, it pushed at the earth that gradually yielded as an act of kindness because it too, having carried you for twenty-four years, having felt you running across its skin, had learnt to value you, to cherish you, to love you enough to shatter the laws of celestial mechanics and return to that evening, return to the previous day, rediscover the setting sun, turn back time to the precise moment you'd wrapped that scarf around your neck, letting you return to the living room and the car, and allowing the train to pull into the station again.

It was now daylight; the sun was out and the mercury was suddenly rising in those mahogany barometers that bric-a-brac dealers offer customers in search of nostalgia when they've run out of Empire clocks to sell.

"I'm boiling, Hippocampus."

The gate had shut again, like the slab on a tomb that was slightly confused about the day, the year or the date of an anniversary. For the first time since it was invented, time had consented to being pushed around and to giving one of its customers a second chance. God, after all, can save those He wishes, and He's no more answerable to scientists than He is to angels or saints.

"Gaston, we'll get this stupid woman out of a tight corner."

Now the clock had rewound to the preceding day, a blank sheet, still to be lived through. All you had to do was bite into the scarf to rip it apart, or simply discard it like an old hanky. You'd finally decide to break up with suicide, that depraved lover who'd done nothing but sink his fangs into your neck all your life, drinking your pain like a vampire.

My poor darling,

So you're still scribbling, my charming scribbler? Tinkering with sentences, pacing up and down your book like a country bumpkin in his scrap of a garden? What on earth are you going on about? Who are these people? I can't hear you!

I can't hear you, don't you get it, I can't hear anything any more. Do you think death is like a music-hall? That we're listening to folk singers down here? That we're laughing at your stories so much we're dislocating our jaws? Do you picture us weeping over the elegies we're stuck with, while the wretched females in your novels are just there to fuck with? You do amuse me, poor sweetheart, with your collected works, spinning them out every night on your keyboard like an eight-year-old showing off his little willy!

Listen to someone who's lived, someone who's fought, someone who's been crushed, someone who's dead. A deceased woman, after all, has the right to freedom of expression as much as any other young girl. I loved you, that much everyone knew; but just as the cuckolded only discover their misfortune when it's too late, you only learnt my secret on the day of my funeral.

Of course, I did confide in you once or twice, jokingly, in passing, so you wouldn't take me too seriously. There are some women, you know, who make the men in their lives believe they're casual lovers, friends lost within swirling herds of relationships.

"I loved you so very much."

But I wasn't stupid enough to run the risk of you knowing. No, she's not daft, our Apple Charlotte! What would you have done with thirty thousand tonnes of love? You'd have been squashed, like an ant under a soldier's boot. You were never more than merely a man. Too much love gives men a hangover.

It's only right that you didn't melt like a hailstone when I showered you with my warmest kisses. You can rest assured I'd often have preferred to love someone else. A moron, an ugly big lump, an illiterate hulk that even fatsos would spit on.

I loved you so much that I forced myself to love other men at the same time, so you'd think I wasn't in love with you. I played at being the girlfriend, the will-o'-the-wisp, setting the bed alight and scarpering in the morning while you remained fast asleep, as stiff as Dracula in the depths of his crypt.

"I couldn't give a damn."

I knew you were not like the mirror in a lift: you couldn't see the traces of tears in my eyes, neat little tears, the tears of an airhead leaving the cinema with her head full of images.

"So you think you're the bee's knees, do you?"

Females falling at your feet. Yes, you: do you think you're the king? With that ego of yours, as bulky as a fridge. But, poor darling, had the puppet down your pants been just as big, I'm sure it could never have penetrated my cleft and, Biblically-speaking, my dearest, we'd never have known each other! Yes, granted, that was far from the case. Now, now: don't go sulking. You're sure to find some gawky lump of a woman who'll compare it to the Annapurna for you.

"You're practically convinced I died for you!"

Well no, my starry-eyed wormsmith, so skilled at your scripting: I killed myself after losing the craft of my cravings. Yes, me, hardly known for my lezzbian leanings, seduced by a schooner and all of her rigging. Surely you knew her, I've talked of her often – my fleeting obsession, fit for short-term romancing. I was so fragile, so concerned about your physical comfort. I was so ill, I was falling. I wouldn't have wanted you to think it was you who pushed me. I swam after her all night. It was blowing up a storm, in the opposite direction to the signal from my mobile, and the schooner continued its journey heading into the wind. My SOS collided with a wall of waves, the words from my messages dissolving into the water.

"And anyway, suicide's a dirty habit, you know!"

People who keep biting their nails end up with none left. You've been so attentive since I played my little game of hangman. You've almost fallen in love, and how tender you are. No, honestly, you've really gone and melted that iceberg. You could have hugged me closer when I was alive. Written me letters, books, novels. If people only miss you when you die, I'd advise all damsels to wear a shroud in place of their finest lingerie in silk, satin or percale.

"Men are such strange insects!"

What do they pick up with those telescopic antennae they also use to pee with? Do their testicles work like batteries? Batteries they charge up by plugging into us? Do their eyes really see us? Or do they get a vague idea by groping along with their hands? Do they think we're tunnels? Or dim galleries they spend their whole life exploring, wearing headlamps? Do they come and visit us as if they were getting down to the coalface? Are we dark holes? But my darling, I was bathed in sunlight! Have you never been dazzled? And yet, to see you better, I've lit you so often!

Well, at least my gaze seems to have projected some sort of light onto you. I really did have to illuminate you, given darkness kept falling on your ever-changing face, even in broad daylight. Paintings whose surfaces are too delicate to tolerate the light of day need to be well-lit.

"Yet another of your fits of megalomania!"

You now consider yourself a work of art. You're taking advantage of my weakness, stifling my whispering with your voice. My little trickle of silence, the mute words of a dead woman.

I didn't light you up but I often followed you. I'd even moved house to live nearby. I knew how to make myself transparent. I stalked you as though I was your guardian angel.

I used to see you at the supermarket, filling up your trolley with all the grace and finesse of someone chucking rubble into a skip. You didn't buy pasta very often, which I found puzzling. Occasionally you'd get some eggs or a joint to roast for the children when they came to spend the weekend. I loved the way you'd exhale like a sperm whale each time you picked up a multipack of Coke, and your habit of poking your head up like a giraffe to examine infant formula that must have reminded you of baby cribs, now no more than a distant memory from your thirties.

Your credit card would somersault through the air when you managed to fish it out from an awkward corner of your pocket, and you'd have that petrified look when you punched in your PIN as if you were about to launch the entire shop into orbit. Perhaps you'd also like me to mention your jars of mustard, cotton buds and packets of vanilla-scented fabric conditioner? I imagine you'd probably be delighted if the contents of your dirty linen basket, your ashtrays and your most elegant dustbin were revealed at the same time?

"I pressed my ear to the door."

I could hear you pacing up and down the wooden floor, abusing the electric kettle like some old Englishwoman who'd lost her marbles. I heard you drop down on the white sofa in a panic. I heard you chewing over ideas, I heard you writing. I heard you sleeping, I heard you dreaming.

"No, I was in bed and thinking of you."

Well, most of the time I was thinking of something else! I wasn't there to watch your every move. Go and find another nutter if you want someone to enjoy your life from a front-row seat.

"I was waiting for you on the pavement opposite."

I wasn't far back enough to see your windows or you doing press-ups on the carpet, trying to lose the potbelly you'd acquired as head of the family. I gave up in the end, but you were bound to make an appearance some day or other. However hard you tried to hole yourself up like a bear as you got older, aging beasts all need to leave their den sooner or later to go and gobble up an auk. You slouched down the street. I followed: you reached a cross-roads and I saw you enter one bar after another, leaving again immediately through a different door. As if dragging a thread behind you, as if you wanted to string these little cafés together into a necklace. You weren't even drunk – and hardly a tad more hyperactive half a dozen espressos later. I was running behind you, and you finally landed up like a wrecked ship in a *crêperie* where you hardly touched your pancake. You weighed anchor in such a hurry that you took the checked tablecloth and table with you, and went into a sulk on finding yourself, in the middle of your hallway, face-to-face with the waitress reeking of butter who you had sucked up in your wake.

"You're making me say crazy things again!"

There was no *crêperie* in your area and you carried straight on. You were moving too fast, I lost sight of you. I could never tell where you were rushing to next or what you were mixed up in. I went back to my hovel, exhausted. I lay on the mattress in a daze and stared at my bike propped up under the Velux window. I wondered why I wasn't infatuated with your brother instead, a decent but unlucky boy who'd never had the nerve to be born at all. You, the only son: you've always seen the solar system as your progenitor. You, the royal child: your light's been shining for half a century and it's not out yet. You glitter and gleam below stars that were set, at your birth, in a spellbound Milky Way, for you and you alone; they beam like lamps in a tanning booth, gilding your beautiful skin all year round while you weep tears of stardust and joy.

What a weird idea – setting your heart on a man who's able to love himself all on his own, like an army of young ladies. You've always been the only woman in your life. Why bother looking for another? *Ménages à trois* are laughable, and as depressing as orgies.

Dead women are sometimes unfair. I used to call you during the night and you were always there. You'd hug me in your arms and console me for being alive. You were an insomniac and cradled me so tenderly I fell asleep. You were downcast and yet often made me happy. I'd learnt to know you the way people learn a foreign language. The way they learn algebra, or chaos theory.

"Enough about you, the man with the ego!"

Look at the hole I've left behind; caress my empty silhouette filled with nothingness. I took my image with me when I went, cutting it out carefully with my rounded school scissors. My living pulsating image, whose finest detail no photograph could ever hope to capture. I was what people call a young woman full of life; and those overdoses of despair did nothing but highlight my joy, letting it sparkle even more. I've known the unlikely happiness that lies in the depths of sorrow, where the bright light of day seldom shines. When light is no longer something people have the right to demand, it becomes a magical gift. Have you never seen a shaft of sunlight in winter, struggling nobly from daybreak, piercing through clouds packed tightly into hard, grey rows like slates?

"Tell me, my darling."

You know only too well that I can't say anything any more, that I say nothing. I'd love to believe the rumours to make you happy. The rumour that the dead still have enough life to speak and write. We can always dream, and rationalise, and think that if they too are rumours, then other rumours may spring from them – the way one lie leads to another, giving birth to yet more. A woman might refuse to do certain things for the man she loved, but not lie to get him out of a tight spot. Not lie to help him write some ridiculous book in which he sweats blood and tears trying to free her from a grave seething with words, as if he thought he was a magician. It's a minor point, but why can't the most sublime acts of love sometimes reserve the right to be the most ridiculous?

"Just tell me in plain words, don't drown me in some tale about witches."

Where we are we have so many monsters, ghosts and goblins, so much fog, pitch-black dawns and frozen dusks, but most of all we have absolutely nothing. Don't forget I'm an unfounded rumour, not that girl you still expect to meet in the street or spy through the peephole when someone scratches at the door. If you hear scratching at the door tonight, if you hear someone knocking, banging desperately until the hinges break, that's because you're being burgled by some thugs.

"If someone's scratching at your door, call the police!"

And if by sheer chance I were to leave a message on your answering machine tomorrow, you really mustn't forget to throw yourself off the eighth floor. That would always be better than going mad.

"Stop!"

You know very well I'd never have suggested you

jumping out of the window. There you go, chattering away again while I'm perched on my tomb as if on a stage, going to all this trouble to guide you back to wisdom!

You should have come up with a book for me while I still had eyes. I'd have read it in my tiny bedroom while eating Turkish delight. I'd have read it in the sunshine, on Square Beauharnais, instead of *Remembrance of Things Past*.

"Do you remember when I used to read *The Fugitive* on our hotel balcony in Djerba la Douce?"

Dear Charlotte,

I admit I've been exaggerating quite a bit. When you died you were already thirty-four. But you looked so young. There are people who lose ten years along the way. Maybe you were like those cartoon cars that carry on moving after losing a wheel, so long as the driver hasn't noticed. When he does, it falls over a cliff.

You didn't know anyone in Marseille, and you should have gone there for the first time the weekend after you died. Your train ticket was found among your things, along with two tickets for a performance of *Lohengrin* that was sung in your absence on 23 May at the Opéra Bastille. I had no idea you liked Wagner.

You know as well as I do that you didn't die on 7 June but on Wednesday 21 March 2007 at seven-thirty in the morning, while I was holding forth on a national radio station following the announcement of a literary prize. Moreover, as I pen these lines, I can assure you that your sister still hasn't laid any sprogs. There's slim chance of the rest happening: of her getting pregnant with a little boy, of her deciding one day to call him something cute like Pindo that'll force him to work in a circus in later life. I've probably turned what really did happen into a bit of a joke out of sheer habit; but then, of course, spinning a few yarns is the easy option. The uncharitable observer might think I was bending the facts to avoid banging my head against the cold, hard metal of truth. Just as I'm wary of keeping a revolver under my pillow. It's so easy to fire.

Yes, I remember Djerba. We were there during the third week of your last September. You'd get up at dawn to go running in the desolate suburbs around the hotel, along with a whole troop of early risers. At midday you'd abandon me on the terrace of the bar to go for an aquarobics class. I'd watch you raise your leg, jump and reach up to the sky, thrashing the water with your feet to work it into a lather. Your hands gripped the edge tightly, as though you wanted to push the pool into the sea. What a fight you put up, what a struggle, what effort went into swimming, to keep your head above water and carry on guzzling life to the full.

You had come to my place on a Friday morning. You'd brought some croissants. We sat down at the computer. We clicked on Djerba and the internet seemed to whisk us there in the blink of an eye, while simultaneously sending the credit card number into Club Med's coffers. You had only seen the sea once, on a bleak day at Dunkirk, and it was cold and green.

In the afternoon you went shopping for a swimsuit. You

were offered nothing but woollen skirts, scarves and hideous socks.

"They're all the rage in winter."

"You don't go swimming in socks."

"I'm so sorry."

Then you remembered you had a niece who lived on Rue Vavin. A girl of seventeen who was one metre sixty-eight like you and spent her time buying fussy frills and flounces from Zara.

You arrived at her place out of breath, as if afraid she might be throwing out the contents of her wardrobe to offer more spacious accommodation to the woollies and anoraks she'd bought the day before in anticipation of the first snows on All Saints' Day. But a sudden attack of acne had compelled her to shut herself away in the family apartment, sheltered from curious onlookers in the street and dandies from the Lycée Montaigne.

She answered the door with her face plastered in clay.

"I'm ashamed of my skin."

"I need a swimsuit."

The sun was still shining when you got back to Rue de Nice with a large supermarket bag in each hand, filled with swimsuits of all kinds and summer dresses in caramel and chocolate, or colours so acidic you were afraid you'd end up in rags if I ever had the mad idea of chomping them straight off your body like sweets.

You'd been sharing a house since the year before. A vast communal room on the ground floor, and bedrooms upstairs dotted along a passageway like cabins on a liner. A liner that probably wasn't anywhere close to sinking, as some nights you'd come across a rat out for a stroll who'd be climbing an air vent to the attic where he presumably shared his home with the pigeons that woke you at dawn with their cooing. The landlord must have been an animal lover because, despite your complaints, he had always refused to chase them away.

He decided to evict you instead of them in February. Perhaps he was living with a fortune-teller who'd warned him your time was rapidly running out. He would have wanted to swap you for someone whose lease on life wouldn't expire while on his premises.

The next day you had an appointment with the editor-in-chief of the radio station who'd hired you two years earlier as a journalist. Audience figures had been falling since July. She didn't hide the fact that you had a seventy-five per cent chance of being laid off before the year was out.

"We've split you into batches."

You were in a group of four female employees, and only one of you would eventually escape the clutches of the national employment agency. A woman of thirty-nine had been fired the previous Tuesday, even though she had worked away from prying eyes in a little corner sorting out press releases. They were afraid her crow's feet might give the station a reputation for waddling along like a lame duck, because a well-known advertiser on a visit had met her in a corridor and felt entitled to re-negotiate the fee for broadcasting his commercials, his claim being that certain listeners looked just like her.

"And the expected return from older consumers is significantly lower."

After leaving her office you went to the toilet. The tissue paper slid into the bowl drenched in your tears. You bumped into a presenter from a different batch. She asked you whether the ceiling lights hurt your eyes so much you had to wear dark glasses.

"Yes."

Opening your bedroom door in the late afternoon you found a pigeon asleep on the pillow. You shouldn't have left the window open: it had seen this as an invitation. You left the house in a hurry. You thought you could hear the rats that had tumbled from the attic breathing down your neck, taking giant strides, chasing after you in revenge for having just insulted a fellow creature by not letting the bird share your bed.

A thunderstorm broke the minute you set foot in the street. You arrived at my place dripping like a statue in a fountain. All the rooms in the flat were lit, a female singer was chirping away on television, and because you couldn't see me anywhere, you thought that – for some unknown reason – I, too, had scarpered from home.

You found me curled up in the hall cupboard when you opened it to take out a towel. Your look of surprise was clearly a request to know what I was doing there.

"I was scared of the lightning."

You dragged me out of my shelter where a sprained back was holding me captive. I got soaked as I hugged you. We both started to shiver. We warmed ourselves up in the bathtub, adding hot water whenever the broth started cooling down. It wasn't easy making love somewhere so confined and slippery. You plunged underwater several times, and I occasionally found myself in grave danger of bending the part of my anatomy which would be of greatest use to us at that moment.

We hopped our way from the tub to the living room. Now the sky was clear. I saw a passing plane, turned red by the setting sun. By the time I pointed it out, it had disappeared. We watched the news.

"They're really in a sulk."

"They're sentenced to death."

"Now we're staring at someone's arse."

An advert for anti-cellulite cream.

"I've got a bottle of champagne in the fridge."

We drained our last glass watching a debate on artificial intelligence. In fifteen years' time it would be part of everything in our lives, and we'd even feel stupid handling our toothbrushes. Not to mention my computer, which would criticise every sentence I wrote in a falsetto voice before deleting it with a snigger.

"I'll just have to get myself a job as a pencil's servant."

But it would abuse its power and take my eye out with its point.

"You couldn't even control a duster any more."

"Stop it, you're tiring me out."

We went to bed. You fell asleep while I tossed and

turned, dreaming about a sleeping pill. I most probably ended up taking one, and when I awoke around eleven you had already gone.

You spent the next few nights with your new lover. A skipper you had interviewed in August. He was seven years younger and felt he wasn't old enough for a serious commitment.

"Anyway, I'm not that keen on children."

And there you were having resolved, on reaching adulthood, that you'd never have any.

You had a godson who was seven. I can't remember now whether he was named after a fruit, but in any case his mother was called Clémentine. When you came back from holiday you looked at photos of my own children that were lying around on the coffee table. You'd never met, yet I felt you harboured a certain affection for them. Perhaps, in sharing their father's bed, you had spun, deep down inside, an imaginary web of connections with these pixellated kids, like those between an aunt and her nephews.

You'd told me a few days earlier that the skipper might be the greatest love of your life.

"But if you marry me, I'll leave him."

My laughter hung in the air between us before you started laughing too.

There were nights you'd leave the skipper alone with his trimaran. You'd send a message to let me know you were coming. You would talk until daybreak, telling me about reporting from a village of deprived people in the outer suburbs who lived in huts cobbled together from bits of cardboard boxes branded Évian, Vittel or Buitoni. They stole electricity from a pylon for lighting and cooking. You had to get first-hand accounts from people whose fate was particularly well suited to compassionate masturbation.

You found it difficult approaching them and the editor-in-chief was incensed you had so little to show for your efforts. You felt uncomfortable getting them to talk so you could earn your salary, while you were refused the expenses that would have meant you could give them fresh supplies.

"To be honest, I don't have the guts."

I told you the radio station would go bankrupt, seeing as young people aren't captivated by tales of poverty.

"And old people don't give a damn about it."

Poverty was something you had experienced and hadn't liked. All that was left from those days when the Salvation Army put you up at the women's hostel was a little grey coat whose worn-out fabric moved me as much as an old teddy's tattered fur. The building was strictly off-limits to men and the ruling regime dreaded the male member as much as a dagger or a firearm. You once told me you felt like part of a brood of vulvae, cooped up behind façades with windows covered in wire mesh.

"The corridors smelt of pussy."

The story went that in the sixties a lodger had attempted to smuggle in her lover at night. The level of vaginal lubrication in the atmosphere was so high that he'd crumbled to bits before he could even climb the first few steps of the lavastone staircase.

"You're a misogynist."

You admitted you preferred men.

It was light.

You opened the window. You wanted to check for yourself that the whole sky had gone blue.

"I have to be in the office by eight."

You went to the bathroom. You came back wrapped in my torn old dressing gown with beads of water on your neck. You pinched a pair of my Jacquard socks, and a shirt too wide for your shoulders whose sleeves you turned up above the elbow.

"It'll feel like I'm wearing you all day."

"I'm heavy."

"Yes, especially your head."

You kissed me and I hugged you tight. I lifted you and tried making love to you, like in those films where they fuck standing up in the corner of a corridor. You were in a hurry.

"You should have thought about it earlier."

And you ran away laughing.

My poor darling,

As if you thought we were raising geese in the hereafter!
Some might say there's nothing to eat here but nothingness
itself. We're fed by the crows – now there's a flock of birds
that couldn't care less about a recent arrival stealing one of
their feathers to write to a bipolar novelist. I don't have a
single scrap of paper. So I scratch and scribble on darkness
instead. The night wind carries it away.

It sometimes feels as though my coffin has an echo like the
outer casing of a piano. If I were alive I'd hear your words
tapping on the lid, like the hammers on the strings of a
soundboard. You strike a few chords, improvising, searching for a melody. Unless the blood has rushed to your head
and you're trying to compose some kind of opera. The kind
where the rising curtain is as black as the velvet drapes they
used to hang outside the homes of the dead as a sign of
mourning.

I'm not me any more. I've turned into you: a parody of

myself embedded in that voice of yours, taking me out for a stroll, pushing me along like a frozen baby in a pram. You're tinkering with things beyond repair, you're in a race against time. You pretend to believe that books are full of the living.

Do you really think Albertine lived and breathed, before falling off her horse? That Rastignac could smell oysters while dining at the Rocher de Cancale? Or Don Juan knew the scent of a woman? Perhaps Don Quixote heard the sound of windmills? And Madame Bovary had an orgasm in a carriage? Do you honestly think novels are teeming with people?

With me no longer around, you decided your brain would split in two like a paramecium and so you reached for the literary first-aid kit. What about writing to a dead woman? She's a character like any other. And besides, there's no risk of her opening her trap. Not only is my mouth shut, now you're talking instead of me by imitating my voice. You've turned me into a dummy and appointed yourself ventriloquist.

"Words can be used to make mummies!"

So you're vain enough to believe your book is a pyramid for bookshop tourists to visit, where I'm going to lie in rest *ad vitam aeternam*? That, unable to photograph me, they'll learn me off by heart? That the printers will breathe life into me? That sentences rubbing against each other will eventually produce a spark and wake Sleeping Beauty? That once I'm translated into Croatian I'll go and bathe in the

Adriatic, and swim as far as Venice to go paddling under the Bridge of Sighs? Do you think the people hanging around in novels really were born at some point? That writers have offspring, give birth, that the pages are flattened wombs and the characters slip out of the letter O, all slithery and slimy like babies emerging from living vulvae?

You poor old trickster, pretending to be a cheery little nutcase when deep down you know full well you're as rational as a stone. Like those pebbles Athenians used to prove Pythagoras' theorems. My love, you are cast in concrete; you've got a microprocessor in the middle of your head, not Perrault's *Tales*. There aren't any fairies in your bauxite brain and you drowned your childhood elves in a pool of depression a long time ago. You've always shot down your dreams, bumping them off one by one like hostages. You think you'll be able to love one day – but, sweetie darling, knackered old things can never love anyone.

"You hedgehog!"

You porcupine! Spiky old club! Pistol! Bazooka! Toy shop Hiroshima! Burst little Bastille Day banger! You think you're an explosion! A war! A revolution! But you spend your time sucking yourself like barley sugar! You're tasting yourself, lapping up every drop! You like hurting yourself to savour your own blood!

"Calm down, my boy."

Stop spraying me with exclamation marks. Words stimulate you like coffee beans. I'd rather you wrote me sentences flavoured with camomile, lime-blossom and hawthorn. Don't forget, graveyards are gardens where the dead kill time under marble gazebos. We can rest at last; we've finally turned our souls into little cushions, pillows to fall asleep on. Where we are there's no more light and no more uproar. It's no longer hot and it's no longer cold. The weather is just fine, to be honest, because it's no longer anything whatsoever. We've no mouths to speak with and no organs cluttering our thick skulls. We're dead – and yet we don't know what death is. It's like being a nomad, but a sedentary one.

"A sedentary nomad, what on earth do you mean?"

Do you want to talk about death? Have you already risen from the dead? Did you somehow stumble into it when you were a kid? Then be quiet, you living so-and-so! Pipe down! You have no idea, and never will. You'll die like everyone else and you'll never know a thing.

It's getting late; I need to finish off this letter quickly. If it doesn't go out with the mail this evening, I'm afraid you won't get to read it for ages. The post here is slack, slow and a bit of an illusion into the bargain. More often than not the roads have collapsed, and they're always plunged in darkness. Our rivers are in spate and we can hardly entrust our correspondence to the rare boats that do venture out there. At best it would arrive soaking wet, but more likely it wouldn't get there at all. As for airmail – don't even think about it. The angels' trade union intends to keep a tight grip on air routes and so far it's stopped them being invented here.

One last word before sealing this letter: perhaps you're not as harsh and prickly as you've made me say you are. A lady in my condition brags, and rightfully so, about never having kissed a barbed remark in her life, and not once having shared her bed with a lover as noisy as a war, an explosion or, God help us, a revolution!

There I go again, blurting everything out; it's time for me to go back to sleep, the sleep of those who neither dream nor suffer, like a white shell in my wooden casing. And you, go and trawl through your cherished memories of me for a kiss.

"Place it on your lips as best you can."

Dear Charlotte,

Looking back, I remember your amazement when, in a plane somewhere to the north of Djerba, you put your head in the cabin window and, at the age of thirty-four, caught your first sight of the sea. I can testify that, two hundred and three days before the episode with the scarf, you were really happy.

It couldn't have been far off nine in the morning, and as if you were both meant to meet at precisely that moment, the water in the sunlight, veiled in mist, was the same colour as the iris of your eyes. That blue, slightly hazy, almost fuzzy, dappled with flecks of yellow and gold like the mysterious core of a marble. You were reasonably happy; and when I put my hand on your shoulder, you threw me a little smile, simple but elegant despite everything, like a double row of pearls.

We'd arrived at Roissy before dawn. We hadn't slept. The woman driving the taxi seemed to have drunk as much diesel as her Mercedes. She kept taking the wrong slip road off the motorway, as though she wanted to slip-knot them together into a mesh. She cast her net far and wide, and only missed the crash barrier at the last minute out of sheer clumsiness. We'd never felt so close, both completely convinced we'd die together in an accident. But luckily the steering was acting slightly erratically and refused to respond to the final turn of the wheel that would otherwise have sent us flying through the terminal windows.

Two days before, you had come round for a good cry. You'd ended up making contact with a homeless person willing to talk, but he'd just found a job in an agricultural machinery warehouse and there was a note of hope in his voice. The editor-in-chief had noticed this. She hadn't concealed the fact that the interview wouldn't do you any favours when it came to passing judgement on the different batches.

You'd left the radio station swearing you'd somehow manage to cope. You'd found an old prescription at the bottom of your bag. It was out of date but you succeeded in making a chemist on Place de l'Opéra take pity on you. Leaving the shop, you dumped the box of tranquilisers he'd agreed to sell you in the hands of a miserable young tramp apparently suffering from withdrawal. Then you sweated for two hours in the fitness room at the gym on Rue de Bagnolet, hoping exhaustion would snuff out your pain.

On Tuesday we'd bumped into each other on Boulevard Voltaire, at the Rouge Limé where I was having a coffee as

I read *Le Monde* to try out the new glasses I'd just picked up from the optician across the road.

"They look like ski goggles."

"They're by a Norwegian designer."

"I can just see you doing a biathlon."

I put them back in their case and snapped the lid shut. You ruffled my hair. You were wearing the same orange suit you'd had on when we first met on 21 March 2005, during a signing session at the Book Fair at Porte de Versailles. You died on 21 March 2007 in the early morning. I believe in coincidences and that's a good example.

I was twiddling my thumbs behind the table where, like the other authors on duty that evening, I was getting as drunk as could be expected on white wine in an attempt to multiply the few customers I did have by making me see double. You appeared waving a copy of one of my novels, *Universe, Universe*, which you later told me you sometimes felt you'd written yourself through having read it so often.

"Don't sign it."

You gave me a postcard of a bright red London phonebox. Your contact details were on the back.

"I'd like to have a chat one evening when you're free."

You immediately vanished behind a pack of pensioners who'd scarpered down the aisle in search of Patrick Modiano. I'd already forgotten your face, having barely seen it any longer than Nadar's camera had focused on Baudelaire's. I could scarcely recall your orangey jacket. We exchanged emails for a month before meeting again, in a restaurant on Rue Faidherbe close to where you lived at the time in fifteen-square-metre digs on the ground floor at 7

Impasse Franchemont.

"You'll be fifty in June."

It was almost as if someone had entrusted you with breaking the news. Thanks to Google you'd learnt the date of my birth and got to know me better than I did myself. You'd even unearthed the star chart corresponding to my birth in some far-flung corner of the web. At the end of the day, though, you hadn't been able to draw any conclusions. You quoted sentences back at me, things I'd come out with back in the 20th century and no longer agreed with, and which felt idiotic enough to have been uttered by someone else.

My impending fifties seemed to impress you.

"You won't be old, but you won't be young any more."

I might have replied that I was prepared to float through middle age until my sixties.

"Are you gay?"

I imagine the rare forums where I was the focus of discussion hadn't voiced their opinion on this aspect of my personality.

"I attract gay people a lot."

"I don't think I'm gay."

"You're not sure."

"One can never be sure of anything."

I may have allowed myself to be seduced by a male nurse in 1975, during an eighteen-day coma following an accident caused by a lorry that crushed my 2CV. I got out of it by calling at the top of my voice for news of the Lebanese war, which had broken out despite my absence. I might also have been duped by a woman with a clitoris of monumental proportions which in actual fact was a penis. However, I'd have been excused for mistaking inconspicuous little balls for plump lips lost under the bushy fur that women had no inhibitions about sporting between their thighs in those days.

"But I have my doubts."

For dessert you ordered a chocolate fondant. You told me you could take me home blindfolded as you'd already checked the place out. When we got to my bedroom, you discussed your breasts with me just before removing your bra.

"I hope you don't like big breasts."

Which they weren't. My new sheets were a bit scratchy. Your mouth tasted of chocolate. We quickly got too hot under the duvet. The neighbours above stopped making love the moment we started. I won't bother you with the details, you haven't forgotten that night. First nights are hard to forget.

At four in the morning the electricity meter woke us up. It started throbbing and smoking as though it had regressed into a steam engine. When the man from the electricity company arrived he called the fire brigade. We'd taken refuge on the terrace and left the front door wide open, totally incapable of finding a phone in the darkness where we were starting to suffocate.

After the firemen left we had a breakfast of grapefruit

juice and cold leftover coffee. The living room with its blackened walls looked a bit like a pond.

"We'll go boating."

"The water's not deep enough."

Fortunately the bed had long legs and we were able to make love above the waves.

My poor darling,

As if being dead wasn't enough, are we still meant to be listening to your tales about an electricity meter and a bed on stilts? Do you think reality is like a slum? Some tiny cellar too minuscule to accommodate your mammoth brain? You love imagination and its glitz, which make even the most beautiful of nights seem dull. You feel you have to polish the darkness with your whims, rubbing it vigorously with sentences in an effort to make it shine. Couldn't you have said that, after making love, we quite simply fell asleep?

"Did you really find life so humiliating?"

Pronounce me, utter me as though I were a word full of passion. If you're convinced I still exist, I can't be anything more than a word. Or maybe two, a whole string of words traipsing out of the shower, dressed in freshly-pressed linen, a pleated skirt, pink overalls, a funny bow tie and a little pair of child's glasses as green as a Granny Smith apple. Marvellous words, just so you don't forget I was a marvel too. And try not to big yourself up too much! I've had more than enough of your metaphors. They just keep coming and coming. As if you're scratching your books and these are the lice falling out.

I could – in a manner of speaking – shout myself hoarse by using the chest of an old man kneeling at the neighbouring grave. You're sputtering your spit all over my rage – and I've every right to be angry! And if your metaphors do resemble showers of lice, well, those lice rain down like phosphorus bombs. I'm sorry to say you'll never make progress. You'll always need to write with crutches, or a Zimmer frame on those nights when you've totally lost self-control. Your metaphors hobble along like someone with a limp. You make little drawings and collages. Try writing a real text for once. So your prose could be used for school dictations.

"You really are too vain, too much of a crook to play by the book!"

To write humble, honest sentences, with no ambition other than to entertain and cultivate the reader. Feeding him, giving him pleasure, like a passionate and conscientious lady of the night. Blast! You claim you're master of your art.

"Well, don't forget to be a tart!"

Libraries and bookshops are brothels filled with joy. Flatter your customers, lick, suck – your mouth isn't the Blessed Sacrament after all! Tell them they're attractive, they're in love and the world's a beautiful place. Instead of a mirror, offer them a watercolour. A pastel. And please, no more of those etchings that only make humankind look like an entrenched camp besieged by barbarians. Compliment them on their prowess, tell them they're about to climax and happiness lies in store. And don't forget to tell them I'm not dead. Because, even if I were, graves are places full of hope where the bones live it up just as much as the ashes.

"In stations, even display cases are on the game."

Dust jackets and book covers expose themselves behind glass like their female counterparts, the whores of Amsterdam. They lay bare bits of their soul on TV and radio, like a hooker flashing her breasts, tempting clients into paying and going up to the bedroom to peruse the rest at their leisure. In any case, I'll have you know that literature must be elegant enough to please. Pleasing, lying, you have to lie if you want to please.

"Lie, my darling!"

Lie, I beg you. Tell lies the way others apply make-up, masking dirty looks with contact lenses as blue as swimming pools, changing sex, colonising brains with slogans as reassuring as old friends. You know very well that truth is basically a lack of good taste; we need to hide our flesh just as much as our arseholes!

"In any case, you're so vulgar!"

Bravo! Thanks to you, I'm seen as a fishwife, a slob! What would my mother think? Or our neighbours, for that matter? They're so prudish they dry their underwear deep in their cellars, to hide their poverty and prevent fellow citizens knowing they're reduced to wearing such rags. Besides, this book conceals the miserable truth as well. The dead live in destitution and the words you put in my mouth are idle gossip you're using to bandage up nothingness, a cold-blooded beast that's not even an animal and doesn't have any blood. Anyway, who told you it was cold? How well do you know the creature? Have you had lunch together? Does it share your bed? You make me babble, you make me scream. You're afraid of silence, you're just scared.

"And stop lying."

You lie too much. Forget violence and imagination. And in future treat horror with loathing. You have some virtues; don't ruin them by chaptalising reality to distil some awful home-made brew.

It's a real pity I'm dead. Otherwise I'd trample all over your novel. I'd make you start it over and over again. I'd make you slave away and you'd apply yourself in the end! You'd write a book as tender and smooth as the face I took to the grave. You never talk about the surprise in my eyes and my wide brow where you'd sometimes rest both hands as though you wanted to find out what I was thinking. Who knows what colour I was: black, yellow, red or yellowish-brown like a bread roll. You don't mention the way I smelt of spring, my gentle voice and the fingers that caressed you, fingers whose tips you compared to the pads under a cat's paw. I was flesh and blood, so full of life. My heart was beating, you know that. You pressed your ear to my breast so often to listen to its rhythm.

Well now, I'm starting to close up like a book of magic spells. Try to settle for making a fair copy of life. Simplicity is pretty.

Dear Charlotte,

When the plane began its descent you fell asleep. Perhaps happiness had knocked you out; unhappiness certainly does the trick. Even the jolt as we landed didn't startle you, and you only woke up when the first mobiles began to ring. The cabin crew had opened the doors. As we came down the steps you told me you'd just been on a plane for the first time in your life.

"I wasn't afraid."

We walked the remaining hundred metres of runway to the terminal. We queued up behind one of the clusters of passengers who'd already parked themselves in front of the passport control huts. I lit a cigarette. I kicked my heels impatiently and muttered under my breath about these endless formalities that slowed down tourist traffic.

You put your hand on my shoulder. But, for the first time, it appeared your mind was elsewhere. You were thinking about the skipper. It was as if he'd followed behind and was tacking around us. I wasn't fazed by his presence; I'd always known love stories were complicated, like those delicate double escapements in Patek Philippe watches that I've never understood at all.

"Put your cigarette out."

The policeman seemed satisfied that I'd comply without making a fuss.

"After passport control, the bags."

We waited half an hour for our luggage, watching a carousel that glided calmly past and gave us a fair idea of what eternity must be like. The skipper had faded into the distance; he'd returned to the high seas. Unless he'd mistaken the desert for a wave and was heading for Tataouine. I let out a little cry of exasperation as I threw punches at the trolley.

"Kiss me."

I kissed you fleetingly on the mouth. And then, to give those hanging around us an audio-visual indication of how furious I was, I sent the trolley flying. It very nearly knocked over a woman running after her little girl.

Our bags finally showed up on the belt at the rear of the pack. I observed that at least we were lucky they hadn't dumped them during the flight along with the remains of breakfast.

"And it's windy too."

Three Gracious Organisers wearing T-shirts emblazoned with the Club Med logo were waiting for us with placards outside the airport, as GOs do, funnelling guests towards the coach. During the journey we were given water and subjected to a shower of praise for the wonders of the hotel where we'd be staying, marvels nearly as plentiful as miracles in Lourdes. I looked through the window at the concrete frames of houses under construction since the nineties. They would probably collapse from old age before they were ever lived in by a large family, a lonely couple or a bachelor driven crazy by buying a new telly every month in the hope of finally spotting himself on the news.

"They might as well brand us like convicts."

Because, after all the GOs in Djerba la Douce had welcomed us around the pool (applauding us like lottery winners with smiles so dazzling they threatened to explode in our faces like gushing torrents of semen), we were directed towards reception where, after taking an imprint of my credit card, they fixed an orange plastic band around our wrists. We were meant to keep these on day and night, for fear of being banished from the village by club-wielding guards dressed in black who kept watch over the beach and gardens to stop locals getting in, catching a whiff of the buffet and getting drunk on the smell of cocktails.

"Their biggest nightmare is someone making off with the sand."

"They've got palm trees."

"They look like feather dusters."

Our room had two beds, or rather two mattresses laid on whitewashed cement bases. There was no question of bringing them closer together to make it easier for our souls to unite. Perhaps this was a way of inviting couples to enjoy a chaste night of slumber after a whole day of sport and heavy drinking, overwhelmed by sleep like Stakhanovites exhausted by fifteen hours of work in the salt mines.

"There's no bathtub, just a shower like in a cell."

"You can see the sea from the balcony."

"It's a long way."

You put your dresses on the hangers in the wardrobe and arranged your toiletries on the shelf above the basin. You were silent while I mouthed off at the air conditioner that was spluttering a bit and the ceiling that felt too low. And I wasn't exactly overjoyed about my body aching after a sleepless night, nor my foul temper which I'd gladly have swapped for a moment of oblivion.

I watched you undress. I could see your bottom in the mirror plonked on the wall above the desk and your breasts wobbling in front of me. The thermostat shut the air conditioner down, deeming it a bit chilly. Not a sound could be heard, other than another couple's whisperings seeping into the corridor like a draught. We made love.

You accused me of scratching you.

"With your devilish nails."

"We're going for a swim."

"We've got loads of time."

"No, we haven't."

I harangued you so much that, when you got up, you were still in a daze after a wretched attempt at taking a nap. Next stop: the bathroom. You slipped into your swimsuit in an instant while I leapt into my trunks. Then we tore downstairs and dashed across the scorched lawn to the beach.

I swam. A sort of hyperactive, uncoordinated crawl, scarcely more efficient than breaststroke. When I emerged from the water you were already stretched out, dripping wet, on one of the low-slung white plastic sun loungers that were lined up on the sand where they couldn't be seen. We'd forgotten to pick up towels from the cabin by the pool where a woman imprisoned within four planks was dishing them out through a hatch with a weary hand.

"We'll dry in the sun."

"We'll be covered in salt."

I'd taken a few pages of my manuscript along with me in a folder. I crossed out sentences viciously with my pen, as though I wanted to smash their faces in. I read out a paragraph that moved me so deeply I was annoyed to hear you laugh.

"I didn't laugh."

"Well, I wonder who did then."

"That girl over there, the one selling necklaces."

In fact, the folder had remained upstairs in my briefcase and we'd barely dipped our toes in the sea. We dried ourselves on a towel someone had left behind. You even asked if there was a cure for scabies nowadays.

You wanted to go to bed.

"If you fall asleep now, you'll wake up in the middle of

the night."

We went to the bar for a coffee. And anyway, you had an aching molar that would have prevented you sleeping. The day before we set off, your dentist, who was furious to discover he'd be subjected to a tax investigation, had done root canal work on it while stamping his feet with medieval ferocity. You went up to the room to take some aspirin. You came back in a flowery dress, with a bottle of sunscreen that you rubbed into your skin in the shade of the trees.

You told me about your psychoanalyst.

"He charges a lot more than my dentist."

He really was hacking away at your salary in return for two appointments a week. He would see you very early in the morning in a brick building on Rue Daguerre. It was so early that each time you half expected to find him still in pyjamas, a croissant sticking out of his mouth and his cheeks lathered in shaving cream.

"In winter it's still dark."

Lying on the couch, you'd focus on the desk lamp that lit up his room. All through the session you'd let your child-hood resurface, bound up in little parcels of words that he occasionally attempted to unwrap, but without the enthusiasm of excited kids opening presents piled high under the Christmas tree. You'd embarked on a quest for wonderful memories, treasures, a tale in which you were a little princess dazzled by her royal daddy. But you couldn't avoid ending up on the platform at Vierzon station, running behind your father who was lurching along like a drunkard, as if he wanted to lose you among the sandwich carts and all those people left exhausted after Sunday banquets at close relatives or distant nephews; they were now rushing back to their homes on the outskirts of Paris, to wash up the breakfast things they'd decided to leave on the dining room table at daybreak rather than risk missing their train.

He was merely a biological father. That's what they call the sperm-filled vials women used to produce children they didn't have the patience to love. You were yet to meet your stepfather, the man who would become, in many ways, your father for life. You were nine when your mother remarried. For a long time you fraudulently used her new husband's surname, just as Balzac added a *de* in front of his own. A few months before you died the Ministry of Home Affairs finally granted you the right to use it. You showed me the letter with all the pride of a woman in days gone by who, after years of struggle, has managed to get her lover to marry her; she's shared his life for so long but always called herself *mademoiselle*, as young women or whores tend to do.

"It doesn't hurt any more."

A tooth can always be fiddled with, but despair isn't like pulpitis. Even if your psychoanalyst had been a surgeon, he wouldn't have been able to wrench it out of your brain with a nerve-broach or forceps. Nor sort through your neurons the way they sift through the spermatozoa in dodgy semen before insemination, so as to hold onto the strongest and get rid of the lame, the disabled, the ones that would in any case have ended up in the support vehicle before they could get to the ovum, or colluded in the birth of some pathetic, uncompetitive individual, unable to thrive and lacking in energy – had they managed, despite their handicap, to overtake all their competitors before the finish line.

On the other hand, a good chemist might perhaps have succeeded in shedding light on the darkest areas of your psyche. A black flag can easily be turned white by immersing it in bleach. You could then even soak it in a bucket of grenadine to make it look good and wave it around on days when you felt cheerful, carefree or just plain idiotic.

So I suggested you'd be better off going to see a psychiatrist instead. With a handful of lithium, antidepressants and antipsychotics, he'd bring your neurotransmitters into line, lighting up your neocortex to such a degree that by the end of the treatment your forehead could function as a lamp and allow you to finish reading *Time Regained* in the dark without waking the person sleeping next to you.

"I don't like psychiatrists."

You got up. I watched you run off towards the tennis courts and disappear on the other side of the wire fence.

I ordered another coffee from the open-mouthed waiter, who wondered whether I'd spat in your face or slapped you with the back of my hand so surreptitiously he hadn't noticed.

You had no epidermis left, your last bits of skin had peeled away long before. Life had not tanned you, life had burnt you like the sun. Some skins are so fair that even the faintest glimmer roasts them like cobalt rays. You belonged to that part of the human race which life will never tan.

I hadn't tried to catch up with you. I lacked the courage, and the love. I'm one of those people who didn't love you enough. One needs to be bold in love, and all you've had from me is the cautious affection of a coward. I was probably afraid of falling into a precipice, a crevasse. There was an abyss within you, and you were built up all around like the sides of a well. You were clinging onto the edge with both hands, but sometimes you'd lose your grip and vanish. Then you'd find the strength to propel yourself forwards again and reappear in your entirety, all the more radiant for having just travelled through the darkness. In the blackness you weren't dead, but you weren't particularly alive either. When the light shone on you again, you had an extra little sparkle in your eyes. You knew that for some people, in the span of one lifetime, those moments of truth are rare indeed.

I'd refused to let you into my rowing boat. It was already too heavy. I'd sailed on too many liners, freighters and old tubs that had succumbed to storms or sunk to the bottom of the sea in fine weather, without warning, as if they had suddenly turned into stone hulls packed to the gunwales with rocks. The story goes that, to prevent the *Titanic's* lifeboats from taking in water and disappearing into the depths of the North Atlantic, the sailors hacked through the fingers of people who were still afloat and clinging onto the sides in an attempt to climb on board.

I wasn't ready for a love story. I was lonely enough as it was and it seemed to me that separate lonelinesses didn't magically fade away when married together but rather inter-bred all the more over time, producing endless offspring when the time came to break up. My illusions had been shattered by successive bouts of bleeding. I'd become cynical because I'd been bled dry.

I only saw you again at the end of the afternoon. I went into the room. You were lying on your back, eyes wide open. You looked like a recumbent statue. Like a stone figure stolen from a cathedral by an eccentric, some oddball seeking the gloomy pleasure of spending his nights next to a facsimile of an *infanta* or a princess. I lay down on the other bed.

I told you that in forty years you'd bring me oranges in a home. As for you, you'd be a smart woman in your seventies with a craving for youth, squashing your wrinkles like blackheads every morning and putting on your make-up with state-of-the-art software that you'd rub on your face with cotton wool. I would envy your independence and your body which would seem so agile compared to mine; you'd trundle me along the corridor muttering *chuff-chuff*, to give the illusion that Ferrari had grafted a six-cylinder onto my wheelchair during the night.

I'd be jealous of your sexuality, sensing its vitality whenever you mentioned some new brand of tingling condom, or hitched up your skirt to show me a fluorescent suspender belt you'd won the previous day at the fair after bursting three balloons in a shooting gallery. I'd have two rotting feet, one arse cheek in the grave, and a shrivelled-up penis whose tanned sheath would be wrapped around the glans like a crumpled wimple – one that even the most slovenly of dirty fat pigs wouldn't use to wipe her piglets with.

"And some day you'll follow my cortège on your bike."

"No, I'll be swimming, you'll be buried in a sewer."

"A bloody crap funeral, to be blunt."

Sometimes we both burst out laughing as we fucked. Had the room laughed with us, it would have exploded in a shower of masonry and – faster than liquid hydrogen – hilarity would have carried us off into space where, changing galaxy as easily as you would a shirt, we'd have presented a terrifying image of the human race to stupefied extraterrestrials on their planets.

Calm returned, there was silence. You told me that, from my point of view, you'd never grow old.

"When I'm old, you'll be dead."

We went for dinner. We walked along by the sea to reach the restaurant. We passed couples who looked down as we approached and friendly GOs who seemed to be walking behind smiles thrust in front of them, as though they wanted to offer us their jaws as a gift. I thought it was a shame they didn't have a couple of horizontal buttocks like a pair of lips. If they did, you might have believed they were hiding an extra smile under their Bermudas for when they happened to turn their backs to us.

During the meal I offered a scathing review of the tomatoes. Some were too squishy, others too green because they hadn't been given enough time to ripen. I compared the gentle sound of waves in the distance to lift music. It would have been enough simply to press the snout of the cold salmon displayed on the appetisers counter (a hapless creature that calmly allowed diners to rip off large chunks of flesh with their forks) to send the restaurant to the third level down. Then all we'd have left to do was take the first metro, change at Strasbourg-Saint-Denis and get off at Charonne for tea on the terrace facing grey roofs and the few apartments still lit in the tower blocks. We would spend the night in my king-sized bed, a world apart from our monastic cell and its mattresses.

"I hate holidays."

"I'm going to get some cakes."

"They're probably too sweet."

I continued my rant, shaking my head as if to deny the reality I'd been unwillingly immersed in since birth. A nervous young girl stared at me, not daring to bite into her lamb brochette and holding the skewer like an ice lolly. You returned with some little crescent-shaped delicacies. I pointed out a hefty couple not far away who were drowning in a sea of plates filled with brightly-coloured grub.

"They're stuffing their faces like pigs."

"They're hungry."

"They look like dustbins."

Especially the guy. He had opened his mouth wide to let food down, the way a rubbish bin swings open when you squeeze the pedal with the tip of your shoe. While I'll readily concede he was a living, breathing example of *Homo sapiens*, his appearance didn't make one feel very flattered to belong to the same race.

"These cakes are delicious."

"They're just cakes."

"They have a lovely taste of orange blossom."

We went back to our room. You stopped on the way to fill your lungs with the evening breeze. I took your hand. It was limp and I let go immediately. Perhaps the truth was you'd only stopped to see whether the skipper was cruising offshore, his sails almost phosphorescent in the moonlight. I, too, felt as though he was hanging around you, and you were increasingly desperate for him to carry you off.

During the night I came to hassle you in your bed. You told me you felt sleepy and dozed off again. I was left grumbling to myself on the balcony before scribbling a sentence in a notebook, a sentence I've never read again and can't remember in the slightest. I went to lie down under the air conditioner, which sprang noisily back to life the instant I slipped under the sheets.

The morning was over. I was dozing in a corner of the beach in the shade of the trees. You woke me with a kiss on the neck. You'd secretly got up at eight. You were tired after running and swimming all morning. Your hair was flat and slick, and made you look like you'd just got out of the bathtub after plunging your head into soapy water.

We went for a glass of punch but at the last minute you chose a papaya juice. For several months now you had been avoiding drinking, smoking and those chocolate bars you would normally wolf down in a trice, the ones you used to buy in threes from the Arab grocer. You were trying to coax your body into becoming your ally: someone to help you bump off the armies from that region within you that still refused to make peace with the natives, and would take advantage of the slightest breach to launch an invasion. That painful region which, ever since its creation, had been reduced to clamouring for your death, because that was the only way it could perish as well and so end the suffering that comes from such deep despair.

There must have been a skirmish on the border. A bit of your cheerful self had suddenly fallen off. It was as if it had tumbled into your glass, where you were contemplating it with nostalgia. You put on your sunglasses. You told me you were anxious about having to go back to work the following week. The different factions wouldn't support each other and guerrilla warfare would break out within each batch. People had suggested you should vent your hatred as an antidote to the distress of being laid off, but that hatred filled you with fear.

"Plus I've had enough of stalking homeless people."

"All you have to do is suggest making a programme on beetles."

"I'm going to have to wear knickers again."

You only wore them for work, though no manager had ever asked what might be smouldering under your dress or in your jeans. During weekends and holidays you liked to enjoy your freedom by taking a break from those cotton cages that only needed a padlock to turn them into chastity belts.

"Wild animals don't wear knickers."

A GO came to ask whether we'd take part in the beach volleyball competition that afternoon. I explained I had a
problem with my right shoulder that prevented me from
lifting my arm.

"I'll be there."

"See you at three, next to the pedalos."

I pursed my lips, disappointed you hadn't planned on
making love to me after lunch. I'd have taken a short nap
afterwards and then started to write before going for a
swim, taking a shower, changing and drinking a mojito in
your company with the certainty, in my heart of hearts, that
I'd truly made the most of the day.

For a long time now I've been a robot. There's a sort of
programme installed somewhere inside me that's replaced
desire and instinct. It's my survival plan, my centre of
rotation, like a trapeze bar for an acrobat. I tie myself to the
end of a leash that I hold in my fist so as not to get lost. You
could get disorientated in searching for yourself every-
where, like a pet wandering all over the place, and there
have even been cases of abandoned owners who've gone
mad.

We went for lunch.

"I hope they've got new tomatoes."

But they were cousins of those from the day before.
More oblong than round this time, yet once again either
squishy or as green as an avocado. We shared our table
with a family of gangly individuals blessed with countless

bones. These people would have given any medical student ample opportunity to revise his anatomy lessons while stuffing his face.

The sea bream *a la plancha* were unfortunately beyond reproach, a fact I had to admit when you quizzed me about them. You said hello to a young woman called Ladybird that you had met at the aquagym. We had a coffee with her by the pool where a noisy game of Trivial Pursuit was taking place. You told me later she'd turned up two days earlier with a man who worked on the railways.

"He's already cheated on her in the hammam."

The heat made us abandon her and return to the cool of our room. In fact you had some time before the match was due to start. You lay down beside me. But I could hear the clicking of ship's rigging. The skipper helped you climb up, leaving your huddled body in my arms, and you evidently possessed a carbon copy of yourself that meant he could be cuddling you on the bridge as well.

I took a chair into the bathroom and balanced the computer on the basin. I wrote a story about a couple who'd met at an estate agency and who – having lived together for several years – split up when the lease ran out. You caught me by surprise while I was staring at myself in the mirror, screwing up my eyelids as though I had difficulty recognising myself.

"You could have done your writing in the room."

"I was afraid of waking you."

You kissed me and your lips were as salty as sea spray. I embraced you, and you held me by the base of my penis and laughed, telling me I had far too firm a hard-on for someone of my age. Whether we did make love, or whether you simply made sure I reached orgasm, when you left for the volleyball I was lying blissfully happy on my bed, wearing that little look of satisfaction children have when they've finally had their way after throwing a tantrum at the candy floss van.

You came back around five. I was polishing off a story about a teenager who dreamt of becoming a detective so he could slap some handcuffs on the little red-headed vixen who'd just dumped him. He would have liked to take advantage of her one last time during the forty-eight hours she was kept in custody.

"You don't waste a second."

"I'm stingy with my time."

Nevertheless, I had planned on folding up my laptop when you got back. I'd already got the beach bag ready, and when we'd had a mint tea, we'd go for a swim, now that the sun's heat had abated and I no longer risked getting one of those headaches that could only be cured by a couple of paracetamol.

"You've got a boring side to you."

"Don't forget your Proust."

I couldn't even manage to wind you up. You took great pleasure in telling me your team had lost, the ball had felt too heavy and the net had been too high.

You called me a nasty little brat when I lost your swimsuit

at the bottom of the sea, stealing it off you in one swipe as we played at scuba diving. You shot out of the water like a rocket, so fast that no-one appeared to notice you wearing a new range of womanskin lingerie whose effect was close enough to nudity for a malicious spectator to confuse the two.

You wished I'd gone for the horrid chubby woman with a cone-like chignon instead; she was doing the breaststroke and circling around a buoy, tongue hanging out like some arse-licking pupil sitting in front of her exam script on the day of the civics test.

"She'd have pressed charges for rape."

I bought you a bikini at the resort shop. You were afraid your niece wouldn't like it. You examined the hideous little objects tourists were supposed to take back as souvenirs, ugly trash to tarnish their homes. You gave me a minuscule terracotta beast as a present.

"You think I look like a camel."

"It's a dromedary."

"Yes, it's only got one bollock on its back."

I don't know exactly where it is now. Mislaid under some loose sheets of paper, fallen into a drawer or on an expedition somewhere among the piles of books strewn across my desk and the tables. But it outlived you.

I sang *La Javanaise* during the karaoke session before dinner. I moved myself to tears. I was annoyed at being applauded far too softly by a group of nostalgia-seeking individuals who were old enough to have heard Gainsbourg tickling the ivories at La Tête de l'Art in the fifties. The rest of the audience peered at a little screen fixed to a column, trying to follow a football match despite the sound being turned off and a snowy picture that went blank every time the satellite passed behind a cloud.

"You don't sing too badly."

I thanked you for your generosity, throwing you a glance about as gentle as a whack on the head. You pinched my arm and called me an old diva.

During dinner, the thought of climbing onto the table to sing the aria of the Queen of the Night momentarily crossed my mind. I didn't go anywhere near the tomatoes which had been disguised that evening with mozzarella slices. They were probably taunting us underneath with all their pips. I decided to arm myself with a knife in the battle against a piece of beef with raw nerves that bled in the mouth the very moment one took a bite.

"You ought to try the couscous."

I was wary of this dish, and even more so of the trio of guests who'd just sat down beside us, their blond hair piled high on their skulls making them look like devilled eggs. When I pictured myself stretched out on the dessert table, my belly resembling a rum baba and my eyes like bluish cherries topping a clafoutis that could easily have been my twin, I figured the best thing was to go for a stroll on the beach to take my mind off things.

You followed me. We made love on the sand, under the moon, as though we'd wanted to take a postcard back in our luggage. But it's a vague recollection: perhaps this all really happened the following day, and I even wonder whether at some point you didn't go off to signal to the skipper to go away. He'd got into the habit of docking his boat right in the middle of the lawn, walking behind us slapping his flip-flops with every step, catching up with us, pushing me violently to one side and seizing you by the waist with all the arrogance of a White Russian come to reclaim one of his peasants.

Sometimes he would carry you off, throwing you into a large sailing bag, slinging the bundle over his shoulder and running away into the countryside. He'd tear apart the sky like a worn-out backcloth, disappearing through the gap to the other side of the scenery, of Djerba, of our adventure. Three hours later I rescued you in the corridor; you were flabbergasted, and I'd scarcely laid you on the bed when he came knocking shamelessly at the door. You fell asleep in his arms, leaving me all alone, tangled up in the sheets.

To be totally honest, you hadn't followed me at all. I was bored alone on the beach and I'd gone back to the restaurant. I whispered in your ear, suggesting we turn my freshly-minted recollection into fact.

"I'm tired, I'd rather go to bed."

I ought to have pressed you further, convinced you of the critical need to experience this for real and paste it up afterwards on a section of wall within your memory, like a poster seeking to advertise our passing infatuation.

We cut through the garden to get back to our room. I still

wonder why you chose that moment to speak to me suddenly in a hushed tone, almost a whisper, about the four weeks you'd spent in a psychiatric clinic when you were eighteen.

You had gone in as a plain old bulimic.

"I'd get up again every night to eat and vomit."

You'd come out classified as a suicide risk.

"I'd tried to hang myself with a scarf."

I had thought your idea was ludicrous. Climbing onto a chair to fasten a scarf around the bulb hanging from the ceiling of that dilapidated bedroom, letting yourself fall, and ending up on the tiled floor after causing a short circuit that plunged half the asylum into darkness. It made me think of the golden age of silent movies, and Harold Lloyd clinging onto the minute hand of a clock on a Los Angeles avenue in an attempt to bring time to a standstill.

The nurse had failed to see the funny side of this. She'd given you a shake before administering an intramuscular injection of ten millilitres of Valium. You awoke ten hours later, strapped to your bed.

You were given another injection because you started to scream. You refused to eat for several days. You were put on a glucose drip, and they tried several times to force-feed you a sugary mixture your taste buds still remembered.

"Like hospital desserts."

You were sent back to your parents with a prescription. You lost the will to speak for three months. You would look at words and sentences as they emerged from people's mouths but you no longer made the effort to hear them. It seemed that even the noise of the street was something you could only see. You were carted around doctors who treated you as a manic depressive, a malingerer or a potential schizophrenic, and you were brought back home. You were placed on a chair, like a dummy presumably weighted down to stop it toppling over.

You remembered your life was then definitively over.

"I was as dead as you can be."

When we got to the room you surprised me with a kiss on the neck while my back was turned. You went to bed and fell asleep. My nightly bout of insomnia clicked into gear, as regular as clockwork.

A few hours later it began to get light and the sky turned white. I'd just composed a story that had crashed and burnt along the way. An unforeseen accident, the words lined up on screen like a rosary of corpses with a string made of articles and conjunctions. Admittedly, there were a few minor injuries, and a small number of unharmed survivors, but I threw them in the recycle bin like the others.

A ray of sunlight entered the room. It might have woken you. I pulled the curtains. Some guests who'd arrived off a night flight were settling in above us. They kept on slamming their bathroom door, window and suitcases as though the hinge had only just been invented and they were discovering its virtues and delights for the very first time.

My poor darling,

Do you still need me? Would you like me to lob my voice straight back, as though returning a ball? But sweetheart, we hardly play any sport here. I've neither a tennis skirt nor a racket. Indeed, you don't seem to realise quite how dead I am. I'm dead, very dead, truly dead, dead forevermore.

The living love death, just as children love the wolf. They'll say that it's prowling around, brushing past them; they're practically stroking it through the bars, like divers patting sharks on the nose from the safety of a cage with their hands inside gloves. I've seen the wolf, I have. He's gobbled me up. Watch out, he'll eat you too.

You're making me talk too much. Stop harassing me. Ask some woman passing by to tell you that I love you. Dream up whatever you like about me; I'll never have the lips to kiss you ever again. It feels like you were given a coffin full of letters and punctuation when I died. On condition that you'd form them into sentences, gradually turning them into a book. As if I'd left you some homework for the holidays, or a flatpack novel with instructions glued to the box for you to assemble on a rainy Sunday like an Ikea kitchen.

Try making the most of the time you've got left, instead of pottering around like pensioners in the cellars of their homes. Don't forget, my dearest, you were born a long time ago; don't burn the summer nights at both ends composing the tale of this house with its cracked foundations, which couldn't even withstand an earthquake that had all the force of a butterfly flapping its wings.

"And another thing: I'm not your parrot!"

I'm fed up repeating the rubbish you stuff down my beak with your bare hands. If you're bent on comparing me to a building, you'll just have to do it yourself. Did you really think I'd spin out your metaphor with you, rather than weaving the words of perfect love? Comparing me to a hovel collapsing in the middle of a city, indeed! Why not to some ruined monument, then? Do you think you're an archaeologist? You're busy re-assembling the rubble of my life like the shards of an ancient vase. Would you also like me to send you my skeleton by mail coach? That way, you could piece me together day by day, dressing me up in those old threadbare trousers and the yellow sweater I left in your bedroom cupboard.

"Bloody writers!"

You and your lot, you're nothing but scavengers. You feed on corpses and memories. You're failed gods, and libraries are mass graves. Name me one single character that's ever risen from the dead. Dostoyevsky, Joyce, Kafka and all of that lot, they've led you badly astray; they're thugs, lazy morons, rascals, rogues, louts! They've simply let their bowels do what comes naturally: excreting their lives and times, smearing every one of those sheets of paper, smudging those streaks, as black and miserable as canals where their words lie lifeless, floating on their backs like freshwater fish boiled alive by a heatwave.

"Bleeding spiritualist!"

Don't come the innocent with me. You fantasise about conjuring up my ectoplasm so you can shove me in a coffin a second time, in one of your books sparkling with self-importance and absurdity!

I'm giving you a real earful, but what do you expect: I sometimes find death so annoying. Meanwhile, hurry up and get yourself to bed. You're living life in the fast lane in front of that computer of yours, fiddling away with the keys like an onanist entranced by a multitude of clitorises.

"You're making me say some really weird things again!"

This playing around with clitorises is pathetic. You're not getting enough sleep, you're like those overexcited kids that need cold water splashed on them to make them shut up. Don't push me over the edge. Otherwise I won't write to you any more. Besides, it's not proper for a dead woman to be corresponding with someone from the land of the living. If by chance I were to be convicted of such unseemly behaviour, I couldn't show my face in any of the graves in polite society. I'd have to stay cooped up on my own because of you, like someone who's got the plague.

"Like a dead woman, in fact."

Dear Charlotte,

The new arrivals must have left their rooms to go off and pay homage to all the hinges in North Africa. My insomnia has probably decided to join them, but it'll have abandoned them along the way to torment some lazy so-and-so preparing to start the day with a siesta in the shade of a palm tree.

I heard footsteps in my sleep. I could smell your presence and the patchouli oil you would use to perfume your hair on mornings when you were in a good mood. I could hear you talking but chose to carry on sleeping. The pain from my morning erection was acute. It felt as though my penis had turned into a cactus with inward-pointing spines. You'd be right to point out how outrageous this comparison was.

I finally woke up.

"It's twelve-thirty."

Waking up, semi-comatose. Your dress stood out like a red stain. I sat up in bed. You were holding a cup of coffee you'd got from the bar between two fingers.

"I've been trying to wake you for a quarter of an hour."

"It feels cold."

You dropped the cup and it smashed on the floor. You put your hands on my shoulders. You pushed me gently.

You made me lie down. You got on top of me. Your body, pulsating and warm, but which at that moment felt rigid and heavy. Your heart beating so rapidly, as if in a panic. That wasn't sweat glistening on your face; you were choked with grief. You put your hands around my neck. You didn't want to kill me, you were pleading with me. Had I loved you even more, perhaps I would have granted your wish.

Your corpse would have been brought home on the same plane as me, a common strangler handcuffed between two stony-faced policemen. A passenger wearing old slippers and running shorts would have pointed me out to his wife (who'd be all turbaned up like a clairvoyant) with his chin, indicating a writer who'd become a criminal just by talking about crime. The day after the tragedy some expert on television would probably have explained how the reptilian brain had always caused the greatest harm to civilised man, seeing as lunatics and murderers continued to be ruled by it to this day.

Hanging our heads, we left the room without uttering a word. Despite being guilty of nothing whatsoever, we felt like accomplices who'd together come up with the same devious plot. After wandering around the pool two or three times like lost souls who might have mistaken it for a font, we sat down in deckchairs.

"I can finally have a hot coffee."

"I really wanted to die."

"At least wait until we're home."

"Bastard."

"Have a punch."

"No, a tequila."

You drank several and I had a load of coffees laced with brandy. I tried tickling you to make you laugh and rediscover your *joie de vivre*. You wouldn't let me touch you so I chased you onto the beach. We didn't have our swimming gear. You undressed and jumped into the sea. I followed your example under the watchful gaze of an aged, sixty-something baby with a smooth face and reddish skin who glared at me with disapproval. My manhood was clearly not making much of an impression.

"If you want, I'll go and get another one from my room."

"I'm calling the GOs."

A guard dressed in black caught sight of us. He ran towards us, blowing his whistle like a prison warden. We were getting further and further away. You were swimming too fast. You began to get tired. You clung onto my shoulder. Then you burst out laughing. As if the tickles had caught up with you. You began to take in water and suffocate. You let go with a fit of the giggles. You were starting to drown.

The skipper didn't come to your rescue: I'm the one who saved you. Ever since the children were small, I told them I wished I could have saved someone from drowning and got a medal. My dream was to come true years later – but the resort manager didn't award me a thing when we found ourselves in his office at dusk, the result of an invitation we'd found on your pillow when we returned.

I brought you back to the beach. You emerged from the

water without the doctor (who was on holiday and had rushed to give you first aid) having to subject you to mouth-to-mouth by pressing his white lips, smothered in anti-UV lotion, against yours. An indignity they hardly deserved. As soon as you could stand I took your hand and we scarpered like riffraff. I've never quite understood how the formal request for us to appear before the Central Committee at nightfall could have got there before we did, nor why it was left on your bed.

Like school pupils caught red-handed and summoned before the head prefect, we went off sheepishly to see the manager. He was wearing an Indian chief's headdress and the regulation smile he automatically put in like dentures when he woke up, contractually obliged to leave it glued to his mouth all day. He apologised for the feathers that drooped on either side of his head like dead ducks.

"I'm playing Geronimo tonight."

At the Cabaret des Dauphins, in a play called *Tipi, Tipi* written by a learned GO who'd died of rabies in 1994.

"He refused to take anti-rabies serum, and we respected his decision."

With his banana-shaped arc of pointed teeth stabbing at his words as though he wanted to tear them to shreds, it was tempting to think he'd administered the bite himself. He asked whether we'd found happiness in Djerba la Douce. You told him you had. In my case, things were more complicated. It would need several weeks of analysis to calculate the weight of my joy, and misery, not to mention a load of anxiety-ridden lead and other heavy metals. My answer was non-committal.

"I'm sure I have."

A GO dressed as a horse came charging into the office.

"They're waiting for you to rehearse *Tipi*."

The manager nodded before flashing his teeth to inform us that, as this was a family-friendly place, naturism was discouraged within the resort.

"Moreover, you're repeat offenders."

He showed us a snap taken the day before by an enthusiastic guest. You could be seen emerging from the water, and it would have been hard to confuse your naked form with the latest style of swimsuit made from softest woman-skin.

"If you do it again, you'll be sent back home at your own expense."

Then he trotted off, holding the GO firmly by the bridle.

Yet another made-up recollection. Forgive me. I've got into the habit of turning my memory into dreams, amusements, jokes. I often find the past feels a tad grey, like the very matter in which it's stored. And what's more it's full of holes, and could be mistaken for lace. I'm not mad on doilies.

During dinner I vented my anger on the tomatoes again. You'd grown tired of listening to me abuse them and went off in search of Ladybird, who was arguing at the back of the room with her railwayman. Each of them took you to task, batting you from one end of the table to the other.

You threw me a look full of concern, verging on panic. I went towards you but couldn't wrench you away from Ladybird, who was now bathed in tears and wiping her face on your sleeve with a circular motion like someone drying a plate so as to leave it shining like a mirror. You tried in vain to speak to me, because she was hugging you tightly and squashing each of her dripping cheeks in turn against yours.

I left you with this couple in their hellish suffering. As I was passing the shop, I saw a man fall from a hotel balcony. He got to his feet and limped in my direction. He told me he often lost his balance after he'd had too much to drink and craned his neck to breathe in the evening air. The medical centre was closed so I helped him clean the gash on his forehead with water from the pool.

I told you about this incident later on in the bathroom; Ladybird had left you drowning in grief and you were dabbing yourself with a towel to mop it all up. You brushed me away with a weary hand as if I were a midge.

"Don't talk such rubbish."

You were right. The man had come out of the shop with a packet of cigarettes and simply asked for a light. He had a Brussels accent. He was wearing frameless glasses. He was tanned and had a pale-coloured patch of skin the size of a metro ticket on his forehead. I could clearly see a deep scar on the arch of his eyebrow, but nothing would have led me to think this was due to a fall – one that in any case had happened some time ago and which I hadn't witnessed myself.

"I made a mistake."

You sat down on the balcony in the dark. You stared at the sky. The skipper must have been roaming around high above the beach, the sails on his boat like the wings of a bird. I went over and touched your hair. The boat fell into the sea. Its sails now turned into fins, and it sped off below the waves to Spain.

You told me that as Ladybird and her railwayman were leaving the table they'd split up. You had said she was welcome at your place, but she'd decided to try her luck at the nightclub. I suggested you join her.

"I'm tired."

You went to bed. Sleep could no longer conquer your fatigue, now immune to any form of rest. Sometimes you wished you could fall asleep for a hundred years, or at least carry on sleeping for the rest of your life. A kind of death – but one still connected to life through the possibility of a distant awakening, just enough for it to stop short of death in all its grim finality. You were convinced you'd be happy; and yet you felt this happiness was so fragile you wanted to preserve it in the icy depths of sleep, to stop it crumbling away when exposed to the open air.

Men feel jealous when faced with a sleeping woman. Even men who don't love enough to experience the pain of imagining her in another man's bed. They begrudge women for not whisking them off too, and leaving men all alone on the tarmac.

I switched off the lamp. I lay down. I called Paris, but all I got were the voicemails of people who were also in bed. I got up, groped around to find my box of sleeping pills, and swallowed a couple with a swig of water straight from a bottle lying abandoned on the floor in the rectangle of light seeping through a large pane of glass in the French window.

When I woke up, I found Ladybird in your bed. She was sound asleep in a purple G-string, her rounded buttocks bulging on either side of the cord, her clothes folded on the chair and her pumps at the foot of the desk. I hadn't realised she'd been concealing such impressive breasts under her T-shirts. One of them was squashed under her, but the other was entirely visible; its nipple was as erect as a teat and would have made any connoisseur of breasts want to take it in his mouth.

You entered the room.

"She came scratching on the door at five in the morning."

"Didn't hear a thing."

"She couldn't find anyone in the club."

You tucked the sheet in around her.

"I wasn't looking at her."

"I was afraid she'd catch a cold."

You laughed, and we headed down to the beach.

That night she was able to sleep in her own room. The railwayman had taken up residence in the bed of an Italian woman and remained with her until the end of their stay.

The end of a holiday which, at some point during that fleeting week, I don't know quite when, began to get dangerously close; it was gathering momentum hour by hour, gradually preventing you from averting your gaze and pretending to ignore it like a child who, at the start of September, can see the new school year swooping down on him.

The skipper no longer dared to flutter around the palm trees, plant himself on the lawn, cross the pool or drop anchor like a buccaneer in our room. He was even less inclined to drag you to the back of the cabin to make love, while perhaps watching me through a porthole as I paced around the room; I'd be seething with rage at the sight of you ditching me so quickly in favour of a sailor, a young man whose expressionless eyes were like two buttons with knots of black thread for pupils.

You no longer even bothered to scan the sea. Only the odd cargo ship now crossed the horizon, or fishing boats during the night, blinding shoals of fish with lamps before harvesting them with their nets.

The fear of going back made you more affectionate. You would give me your hand, asking me to keep hold of it. Who knows, our blood vessels might have joined together, and with the mixing of our blood you wouldn't have felt so alone. Perhaps it's that longing to share another person's body, just as one might share the same studio apartment. Two brains fused in one head, hearts side-by-side, becoming each other's better half. Discarding once and for all the solitude we're given at birth, and which we thank our mothers for with a howl and a scream.

Your loathing for procreation had melted under the Djerba sun. One evening, as you sat drinking a daiquiri, you told me you could feel the strange pull of motherhood becoming stronger inside. An intense longing, an incomprehensible desire to be in the presence of someone who owed you their very existence. You'd easily find the energy to bring up your child when the midwife laid him on top of you.

"I wouldn't have any choice."

I asked whether you wanted a boy, a girl or another daiquiri.

"Twins."

Why not, indeed. You could even populate some remote corner of the planet, some brand-new city where you'd fill the streets and buildings. Stocking them with prams, cradles and schools packed with brats squealing in the play-grounds; they'd send balls flying through windows and set fire to the schoolmistresses, to avoid cluttering childhood with arithmetic and grammatical rules completely lacking in appeal.

"Nine months is so very long."

You felt you wouldn't have the time. Life took far too long to germinate inside the womb. You wouldn't have the patience to wait, you'd grow weary half-way through. You'd swell the ranks of those who give up, fickle individuals whose enthusiasm fades as they sense that stranger inflating their belly, that stowaway, that immigrant deep inside whose ways and customs they fear might be intolerable, and that habit of waking the natives in the dead of night while they sleep the sleep of the just.

"You'd never father a baby with me anyway."

Because, even had the skipper changed his mind, and suddenly matured such that he'd agree to inseminate you with his foam, you couldn't bear the thought of having a seafaring child. Some little bobble-hatted sailor, snivelling away because he had to remain at the helm in a storm while you cooked his meal down in the hold, on a filthy stove being rattled around by the rolling of the boat.

"I'm too old."

"If you had a baby with me, he'd be younger than you."

You stifled a laugh, a silent laugh. An aborted laugh.

Time was no longer passing by; it was collapsing like an ice floe with the onset of the Arctic summer. The previous evening you'd been crying at the restaurant. Uncontrolled sobbing, an unexpected sound that gave Ladybird a start. She had joined us blind drunk, her cheek still bruised by the railwayman's hand: she'd lashed out and scratched his Italian woman when she met her, draped across his arm, in the alleyway of the souk where she'd gone to buy a fake Vuitton bag.

She would probably have offered you her ample breasts to siphon off your tears with her nipples, so returning a favour with a favour. But, as though I'd suddenly raised the subject of the psychiatrist again, you knocked over your glass and ran off.

I caught up with you on the beach.

"Don't say anything."

I'm a compulsive talker, but I didn't say a word.

On the morning we left you took pains to sort out your dresses. You ran your fingers down the creases, even calling reception in vain to ask for an iron. You were resigned to your imminent return to the world of work, and before leaving the hotel you slipped on a pair of knickers as a sign of mourning.

In the plane you turned towards me and tugged at my eyebrows, asking why I didn't grow some whiskers.

"You'd look like a grey cat."

You could easily have seen me wearing a cassock too, in the role of a priest taking confession, getting my kicks from listening to young female parishioners as they described their depraved habits; they'd be all hot and sweaty, while I'd be screwing up my eyes behind the screen like a fat tomcat licking his chops. In your opinion, what really got writers excited wasn't so much living as witnessing the lives of others at events like balls or massacres. People like me didn't go to the bother of letting their hair down or getting into fights: they were like those photo journalists who're happy simply taking snaps at shindigs for the jet-set, or in Baghdad markets littered with corpses after a terrorist fiesta.

"What I like about you is your bravery."

You dazzled me with your smile. You stroked my cheek.

You showered me with nervous little kisses.

"You're a coward."

I didn't ask why. You seemed so cheerful. Maybe this was yet another allusion to my lack of enthusiasm for having children, so depriving some little kid in a babygro of the chance to follow my coffin one day.

The in-flight meals were disgusting but you wolfed yours all down, even the fatty white cheese chock-full of sugar. I offered you mine and you gobbled that up too. You wiped your mouth, rolled your napkin into a ball and put it in the cup. You appeared withdrawn. Your happiness had suddenly melted away. You put your hand on my thigh. You stared at me. You'd never looked so wide-eyed in my presence. You seemed astonished that I hadn't changed my seat, and even more so that I hadn't fled through the emergency exit in a blind fury, like an actor in a farce making for the door. In a hushed voice, you took back every one of the words you'd just uttered. Gently, as if pulling out spines, one at a time, from the buttock of someone who's sat on a sea urchin.

When the stewardess made her way along the aisle selling duty-free, you bought me Habit Rouge by Guerlain. The plane landed at Roissy. The taxi dropped us off at Rue de Charonne. You came up with me. You could sense I wanted to be alone. Still that obsession with retiring into my cave, perhaps out of fear that others might unduly influence me, like those Southerners who dreaded their daughters' complexions becoming darker if their nannies, black as ebony, were to accidentally quench their thirst from the same cups.

You suggested we have dinner together the following Thursday. You were keen we both complete the customer satisfaction survey we'd been given when we left the hotel. You left, dragging your bag behind you. I shut the door as though closing some brackets. I retreated into my lair.

My poor darling,

Where's my candle? You don't really expect me to write in the dark, do you! I told you in my first letter that the dead don't sleep in boutique hotels. And that's putting it mildly: the afterlife is more like an old inn at best, and a badly-kept one at that. Staying in the last brothel on earth would still be a better bet, even if that meant putting up with the constant traffic of hookers and their punters. The saving grace of this whole affair is that, sadly, none of us are alive any more. A hovel is better than nothing, and I would gladly exchange the softest of nothingnesses for the vilest of nettle mattresses.

You couldn't care less that souls are but flights of fancy, and we haven't even got the flames of hell here to warm our frozen bones. I'd be just as precious to you now as when I was alive if you could conjure me up in your mind. To think I was once a young girl who turned boys' heads in the metro; you know perfectly well that nature has given us women extra faces, hidden under our petticoats and even inside our cosy bodices, not to mention the one with the really broad grin that we grip so tightly between our thighs when riding on public transport.

"And you've turned me into a novelistic device!"

Not even a work of art, a statue or a piece of music! No, a character, if you please! Or, to be honest, a practical tool, an ingredient you fling into your lexical soup to thicken it when it turns as clear as water.

"So cook your stew under your own steam!"

If the pâtés you've whipped up from your sentences seem bland when you sample them with your knife, I'll have you know that I couldn't care less if you sprinkled me all over like a pinch of cayenne pepper.

Poor lad surrounded by pots and pans, busy simmering books that collapse like soufflés. Not only am I shelved on your spice-rack, but with each of my letters you expect me to act as your chef's assistant, your little kitchen boy! You win, I give in. I've always had to give in to you.

"Admit it, there's never been a dead woman as gracious as me!"

You want to know if I got your letter, whether some chambermaid read it aloud to save me tiring out my eye sockets? But of course, my love! We get so terribly bored here in these country cemeteries. We're eager for news from the city. And because, frankly, nothing ever happens to us, whenever it does we're a cackle of constant chatter, like a worship-house of wimpled women, wittering on about wisdom, waffling and waltzing in the Sacred Scriptures of Schmaltzing! We normally arrange a little get-together among our fellow holidaymakers.

"O seasons! O tombs!"

Let's muse over the account of your travels, shall we? My dear tourist! What an odyssey! Having to eat tomatoes for a whole eight days! In the company of a railwayman graced with a sidekick named after the Blessed Virgin's bright little bug! We've been really depressed of late, because all we've had is an undertakers in place of Club Med. And those graveyard GOs in black suits, whose idea of beach volley-ball is chucking us down a hole!

"Why have you splattered paint all over your trip, instead of turning it into a watercolour?"

Do you want me to set the record straight? To say I was happy in Djerba and never cried once? To sweep up your rubbish? Like the grief littered through your prose, those insulting remarks never uttered, and that sordid embrace when I apparently suggested you kill me? When it comes to putting happiness into words you haven't a clue, and that's clearly why you're so mediocre.

"You've been such a disappointment, little master. I regret ever falling in love with you."

Dear Charlotte,

Death robbed you of compassion along with your life. Tonight I'm sorely tempted to finish with you, and forget you altogether. I wouldn't even be that bothered about you storming into my dreams to pester me, mad with rage. I'd see you in the evenings, lying scantily clad on my sofa, but I'd blow your ghost away like a cloud of ash. You'd pounce on me in the shower, but for a girl made of water, soapy lather or fibres from a massage glove, it's not that easy to get a solid erection out of a man who'll soon be (yes, time flies) seventy-eight.

Transforming yourself into alcohol to get me drunk would be pointless: I'd know it tasted of you with the very first sip. And if you were ever vulgar enough to stalk me down the supermarket aisles, you ought to know, my little succubus, that I'd stone you with milk cartons, sugar, cocoa powder and coffee filters. If you still persevered I'd bombard you with honey and fistfuls of corn flakes, muesli and oat flakes.

You'd be a lot less cocky faced with jeering customers, saleswomen and checkout girls who'd left their tills to pelt you with small change.

I don't want to say this again, so let me warn you now: any more of your shenanigans and we're history. I'll kiss you all the same; but this time your cheek will have to do, because you don't deserve one on your lips.

My poor darling,

Really, by now you should know better than to pick a fight with a dead woman! Wanting to drown me in shame in a supermarket! Don't you think the fact I'm no longer alive is grotesque enough? Do you intend laying bouquets of laughter on my tomb instead of chrysanthemums? Will you never give me any respect? Will you never understand a thing? Don't forget, you've labelled me a strangler. Would you like me to reward your slander with a gentle word or two, a tender caress or a blowjob from beyond the grave?

"You've always confused women with spittoons!"

I'm neither your plaything nor your tart! Let your imagination run riot on the living, on women who're able to slap you in the face. As for me, I've no choice but to leave my defence in your capable hands. Thanks to my intervention, you can insult yourself to your heart's content, knowing full well you'll never do yourself much harm. Nobody has ever smashed in their face by themselves, or knocked themselves out with their own fists.

You people, you men of letters, you slip so willingly into

confession; but you'll only admit to the crimes you've heard about because the poor victims were your peers. And that lets you get away with sins that would make you blush like virgins being stripped by a brute.

You little imposter, ridiculing and mocking yourself to show how humble you are. Get down on your knees if you like, grovel all you want, cover your head with peelings as an act of contrition: you're fooling no-one, it's just you seeking more love and adoration, like some idol that's showered with praise, even down to his haemorrhoids!

"So here I am, I've fallen into a pit of vulgarity, and it's all your fault!"

There's not much point to hanging about in your novels: your sentences are stinking alleyways where damsels stumble around in the muck. Why can't I be the heroine of one of those nice clean books, as bright as a new penny, fragrant with the lavender of hypocrisy and the mothballs of fine sentiments?

"A dead woman needs her sleep, and how sweet it must be to start with clean sheets."

Dear Charlotte,

You'll soon blame me for the fact that you only exist in this book. I could well be forgiven for levelling the same accusation at you. I'd rather you were somewhere in Paris, or elsewhere, one of those countries teeming with life compared to the provinces where you thought it was a good idea to make your home of late. There's no pleasure in not meeting you any more, and knowing that when I do happen to glimpse you walking back up the street it can only be a distant memory rising to the surface again.

I'll always resent you for leaving me; some break-ups can never be forgiven. You've proved the death penalty will never be abolished, because passing sentence on oneself means punishing others too. You might have granted yourself one last-minute reprieve, deciding to review your case, sending yourself away to deliberate again and commuting your sentence to life in perpetuity. An accident, illness or old age would, one day, have taken care of your release from prison. One must never lose faith in death; it hates nobody enough to eternally deny them the right to sanctuary.

Death would not have resented you for not leaping into

its arms. Death is a grandmother, seizing hold of children who try running off as night falls. She puts them to bed without telling them off, kissing them just as tenderly as the more affectionate ones who came looking for a cuddle in the middle of the afternoon instead of staying on the beach to play with their pals.

Life is a never-ending Sunday, I'll grant you that. Either people are getting bored, or scraping their knees on the rocks, or squabbling over a spade, a rubber ring or a bucket, or at each other's throats, or happily kissing, or building sandcastles with their backs to the tide. But I imagine that as the day draws to a close. People must be closing their eyes and thinking. These are memories to treasure.

My poor darling,

Good Lord! You're dripping all over! Your waters are breaking! So you're finally falling in love with life! But you're not singing its praises, no, far from it: it's as if you're trying to palm it off on nosy onlookers, like a street peddler flogging a cheese grater! Go on then, live! Stuff your face full of happiness! Get yourself pissed on the bottles of pleasure you hid so well, way back when you could have slung a glassful down my little gullet!

"You're determined never to accept people just as they are!"

Perhaps you'd like to wrench me out of my grave, like a bourgeois philanderer snatching a hooker off the streets? I'd rather you joined me here, tossed on the slagheap! Don't keep asking me to do the impossible, and for once pay heed to reality. Get your skates on: in a few years you'll be too decrepit, and I'll turn my back on you when you die in favour of seducing some tastier young corpses!

Do you think we're that bothered about our health here? That we go swimming at the pool in Butte-aux-Cailles?

Perhaps we keep up to speed with the latest spring-summer collections? Maybe we have our own top models and cover boys? Or could we be avid naturists, flashing our tailbones at the moths? Sweetie darling, you're such a big kid, always thinking the party's never going to end. You'll stop calling me "pussy", which is probably just as well knowing my past allergy to cats. You and I won't visit the woods again, but you'll go without me anyway.

"No, little man, you won't make me dance any more!"

Neither in your bed, nor on your terrace. Even if, deep down, I really do deserve a ballet or a waltz, or perhaps even a Polish *mazurka*.

"And why not a striptease?"

Men are all the more endearing because they're so ridiculous, with their trousers round their ankles while they feel the weight of their genitals – right there in front of our eyes, as if they wanted to humiliate us because fate has granted us nothing more than a trapdoor!

"Yes, a striptease!"

That'll make a nice change from all those tombstone womanisers, those show-offs flexing their vertebrae who only end up jabbing us with the ends of their hip-bones when they try to screw us!

My darling, stop making me splutter up exclamation marks. My mouth feels like it's a crossbow. Our little household has no need to launch itself on arrowheads or hyphens, any more than it does to bombard itself with punctuation. This drama has played out far too long; you know very well that I never went looking for trouble when I was alive. Why do you flare up like tinder whenever I tell you what I'm thinking? You lie, you lie a great deal, you lie too much, and I don't want to turn into a lie myself. Stop shoving me into the darkness of your imagination at every opportunity. Because when I come out I'm covered in soot.

My sad old excuse for a lover, I beg you: if you *are* going to talk about me, then at least give me a walk-on part. Just occasionally, slipping me casually into the text, as though your book were a forest and the fluttering leaves let light filter through. Let me be that light, crystal-clear and sharply-defined; you might as well allow people to see me, let me resemble myself a little, as if I were almost alive, like a photo that's not too blurred.

"Don't gobble me up, don't gulp me down!"

I'm already deep enough as it is within my grave; I don't want to be laid to rest yet again, buried inside some fictional girl. One of those slightly barmy females you treat like bricks, building novels crammed full of your pain.

"Look at me when I'm talking to you!"

Don't squint. You can listen with your eyes too. Oh, and while we're at it, you tire me out! I'm off to bed. Spend the night drinking tea in front of your telly again. And don't you dare wake me up. Tonight I'm not your cheeky little minx, nor some robotic bag of tricks, and I couldn't care less for your prick!

Go on, keep up the pace, little donkey. Carry me gallantly on your back to the end of my story. Like a fair maiden being led to the slaughter.

Dear Charlotte,

After a week spent living together in the sun, I was pleased to find myself alone in the shade of the curtains. I was starting to appreciate solitude more and more. I loved it the way others love parties where the women flow as freely as the Dom Pérignon.

I opened my mail. Among the bills was a letter from a reader. She told me her husband had been cheating on her since February with her housemaid. I didn't know her personally, but perhaps she wanted me to go and reason with this brazen hussy. However she lived overseas, so it was too far.

During the weeks that followed, my live-in lover was Word. I'd only go out to see my children or dine alone in a local restaurant. To top it all I was now sharing my home with two or three mice who were kipping under the sofa and the beds, and even taunted me in the bathroom. They must have had a housewarming party when I was away, and I suspected they might be renegades from the gang of rats on Rue de Nice who had followed you the day before we left for Tunisia. They terrified me as much as crocodiles, and I'd run and seek refuge in the toilet each time I spotted one dashing across a room or frozen on the carpet, staring at me with its nervous little eyes.

I tried feeding them poisoned wheat, but they steered well clear and preferred the rusks I'd find half-nibbled away in the cupboard. I bought some traps, but neither cheese nor chocolate (which I'd been assured by the salesman at the DIY store made the most effective bait) could tempt them.

I contemplated moving house. Unfortunately, the apartments I viewed had a seedy look about them, and I feared that families of dragons might be hidden under their spanking-new wooden floors, ready to devour me in my sleep.

We would chat via email. You told me about your relationship with the skipper. You blamed him for being only twenty-six and wished he'd make an effort to age faster than you. That would have let you both celebrate your thirty-fifth birthday the following April 18. But he displayed such an alarming lack of goodwill that you could already picture yourself at eighty, using your walking stick to drag around a kid of seventy-two who'd be frittering away your cash on ice-creams and game consoles.

He had dropped anchor in Paris the day we returned. It was as though he'd hitched the prow of his trimaran to the tail of our plane. You'd spend your nights on board with him in the cramped cabin, and in the mornings you'd jump from the bridge into the first metro to get to the radio station. The editor-in-chief was devastated.

"Those homeless guys have scuppered the ratings."

Since your return they'd embarked on desperate measures: testing out stories about dogs that had been run over. Your job was to go and interview their teary-eyed owners. You'd attended a funeral for a bulldog. You'd recorded the moment at the end of the service when the police had intervened to evict the hapless creature from the family vault. Someone had gone and shoved it between a grandfather and a nephew who'd passed away in 2003 from hepatitis C.

You would call me.

"We could have dinner on Sunday or Monday, if you like."

When we met up we hardly went to bed, and often never slept at all. The skipper was probably lodged somewhere close to your heart, and might have foiled our plans by bursting out of your mouth like the devil. Above all, though, you were shattered: the strength to carry on living had begun to evaporate, haemorrhaging away, but without blood or wounds, in steam and mist that no-one could see.

Perhaps you were afraid you'd tire me out if you were gloomy around me, so you bubbled with enthusiasm and when I cracked some painful jokes you burst out laughing, like a little girl at the puppet theatre. You agreed to set off on safari through the apartment, armed with a broom. We never did flush out the mice, but we got a fright when we spied some fluffballs under the radiators.

In the evening you would sometimes return to Rue de Nice. You wanted me to see you back home. You gripped my arm, as if someone had switched off the city and you were frightened of getting lost in the darkness. You told me that, two days earlier, the beautician on the ground floor had fallen victim to an act of summary justice when her ex-husband had trashed her shop.

"He even demolished a wall with a sledgehammer."

We both went up to the flat you were sharing. A twenty-something girl was talking to herself in front of the telly in the spacious downstairs room. You were busy moving out. You'd already filled three boxes of books. I climbed up to your room with you. You removed your shoes and lay down. You fell asleep with your clothes on.

I went back home. Before the halogen lamp was lit, the apartment, with its large windows staring out into the night, looked like an aquarium, or a lobster tank in a restaurant that's just closed after the last sitting.

The radio station was losing advertisers every time a dog went under a lorry. You were no longer split into batches. The unions had notified the Ministry of Employment, and the idea had been dropped. Despite this five people had already lost their jobs. According to rumours, the director had drawn lots at the gambling club where he would squander his wages every night playing roulette. You felt guilty for still being there.

You asked me whether I knew a publisher interested in

launching a series of books on music. You had been at the conservatoire. You'd taught the clarinet. You'd sold it the year before to buy a laptop. You never talked about music because you wanted to write a novel. The only work of yours I've read is a short story entered in a competition organised by the Parisian transport authorities. You'd referred to the bus smelling of tangerines one morning, and your submission was probably deemed too libellous to win a prize.

"I'm looking for another job, but I can't find anything."

Now you wished they'd got rid of you after all. Redundancy pay and a few months on unemployment benefit weren't exactly going to set your world on fire. But you couldn't take any more of those nightmares, crammed full of dogs with clip-on mikes around their necks exploding like grenades.

Occasionally, on a Sunday, the skipper would come across you stretched out in the middle of the cabin. He'd scrape you off the floor, and because he probably couldn't find a jar comfortable enough, he would lay you down on the berth.

"He's kind."

You'd have loved to wear him like a lifejacket and you'd have tightened the straps until your bones cracked. You told me he'd surely be the one to save you.

"He listens to me."

Yet sometimes you'd abandon him. At night you would drop the little rubber dinghy that hung on the aft deck into the water and row through Paris. I could see you making your way back up Rue de Charonne: you'd lost your oars and you were battling against the current, paddling with bare hands. You couldn't go any further, and you were ready to charge all the way down to Bastille. I threw you a rope over the guardrail. My arms aren't that strong, but you'd made yourself so light I was able to hoist you up to where I lived on the eighth floor.

You were trembling and your face had turned blue with cold. I made you a pot of Darjeeling tea, tucked you up in my bed and drowned you in duvets, pillows, blankets, and all the coats and woollens I could dig out of the cupboards in the flat.

"I feel better."

I radiated heat, pressed against you like a hot water bottle, my legs wrapped cosily around yours. Your heart was beating less rapidly and I could feel your warm hands in mine. Neither of us was probably that keen on pleonasm, and we didn't sense the need to commit the redundant act of making love. In those moments our passion for each other was so intense we didn't feel compelled to scale the dizzy peaks of orgasm – a pleasure which would have seemed so minor in comparison. Even that spine-tingling sensation couldn't match our blissful serenity. Despite my fear of falling in love, I remember there were times I really did love you.

At eight o'clock you jumped out of the window and swam to the radio station.

They'd given up on those grief-stricken episodes that punctuate pet owners' lives. They had taken a passing interest in the plight of the great white shark whose populations are in steep decline; but, to be fair, this is not the most articulate of fishes and the lack of sound recordings meant leaving its fate in the hands of the trawlermen. Gorillas are more talkative, but their sign language hardly lends itself to anything other than television chat shows.

A few AIDS sufferers had their fifteen minutes of fame in a series of programmes sponsored by a pharmaceutical lab that had developed a drug whose effectiveness was similar to that of a placebo; however, it cost peanuts to manufacture and they hoped to sell billions of boxes to third world countries at a bargain price.

"It's better than nothing."

That was the product's strapline. Embassies representing the further-flung nations protested, and the radio station was threatened with having its frequency withdrawn.

You were given the job of infiltrating the suburbs, and promised a special bonus if you managed to interview a girl involved in the hell of a gang rape. You'd made contact with some secondary school pupils in La Courneuve, but they all cherished dreams of becoming finance traders, researchers or even high-ranking civil servants, and you were suspected of giving a voice to cocaine-fuelled rogues from a cram school in Passy despite their accent. There was some talk of sending you to the mullahs as a hostage. But the fear was you'd be executed before you could send back any recordings at all.

For Christmas, the skipper took you on a cruise to Amsterdam. You shuttled up and down the canals with shortened sails so you'd have time to enjoy the sights and soak up the local colour.

At the Van Gogh Museum you saw *Wheatfields under Thunderclouds*. You thought you really could hear the sound of thunder and, soaked to the skin, you took shelter in the cafeteria.

You liked to lie down at night, cocooned in your cabin, and watch the houses drift by, illuminated by the orangey lights of the streetlamps.

When you got back to Paris, you were practically lost for words when the photo counter at the Fnac store said they were unable to make prints from all the images you'd stored up in your memory.

You returned from Holland with a striped handbag. It features in memories dating back to those few weeks before your death. It was hanging on your shoulder that evening when we both discovered someone had smashed the window of my car which I'd left in the parking area under my block. All they'd stolen was a plastic dog that used to nod his head in the rear window to keep the children amused. Two months earlier someone had ripped out the car radio which, unluckily for the crooks, I had yet to replace.

From January onwards you came by more often. You asked me, as a favour, never to put my mobile on silent so you could always reach me. You called to tell me you were afraid. You arranged to meet at two in the morning in a bar on Rue de Lappe. You ordered a drink, but getting drunk scared you as well. You asked me to drink it instead.

Whenever you didn't spend the night on board after leaving Rue de Nice, your parents put you up at their place on Rue Meursault in the 20th *arrondissement*, in a studio on the mezzanine that your father normally used as a spare office.

"I've found a really nice doctor."

He signed some sick notes for you. You told the editor-in-chief you suffered from back pain that meant you had to remain lying down. During these oases of calm you turned off the engine. You were like a plane that's been returned to its hangar.

"I'm resting, as if I were dead."

You were fond of putting your life on pause like this. Of ignoring the racket and forgetting your days were numbered. At that time you imagined the dead were simply fast asleep. Perhaps you resembled them a little on days when your dreams didn't wake you with a start. In the evening your mother knocked at the door and hung a bag filled with fruit, cheese and *petit beurre* biscuits on the handle. By the following day it had gone.

One morning your parents heard the shower running. You'd emerged all numb from that long sleep, and were coming back to life under the hot water. You went upstairs and announced you'd be thirty-five in the spring.

"I'm going to be a big girl at last."

You were on a high. You asked your mother to make you some pancakes. You ruffled the few hairs that remained on your father's head. You asked him whether he'd prefer to be grand-dad to a Chloé or grandpa to a Lucas. You told your mother to start with the second pancake.

"Because the first one's always a disaster."

There was no milk left so she made you soft-boiled eggs. You buttered some soldiers. You went off with bits of yolk stuck to the sides of your mouth.

The skipper was waiting for you at the corner of the street. His boat was obstructing the traffic. He'd shattered the windscreen of a lorry while dropping anchor with typically Parisian indifference. The driver was kicking at the keel, now half sunk into the roadway. You jumped onto the bridge, and the skipper had to negotiate a sea of vehicles that now stretched as far as Porte de Bagnolet before sailing off into open water.

You'd already reached Chartres when you remembered that, without an extension to your doctor's note, you were meant to go back to work that morning. You had to sail as far as Saint-Nazaire because of the headwinds before the skipper could finally change direction.

You were late. When you got to Boulevard des Italiens you flung yourself into the radio station through an open window.

My poor darling,

Summer is drawing to a close: here come the first leaden
skies of September with their cortèges walking through the
rain. There appear to be more deaths than ever at this time;
we're practically falling over each other in the dark. A
never-ending flow of coffins, bearing old-timers who smash
open their lids one by one, seething with rage at not waking
up in their own beds. They miss the oddest things, like the
smell of the sewage plant that used to drive them mad in the
evenings as they stood at their windows for a spot of fresh
air. They're nostalgic for bouts of rheumatism and flu, even
the very illness that finished them off. They miss it all, right
down to the agony of dying itself, and wistfully recall their
last intake of breath as though it were nectar. You could say
that those who've loved life the least hate death the most.

"Let that be an example to you, you little bastard!"

Stop being unhappy, once and for all. It can't be that
hard: people do give up heroin. Dazzle your blackest
thoughts, the way the Djerba fishermen dazzle fish in the
Mediterranean. Throw them in a sack and drown them in
the Seine. And don't let me catch you getting bored. Don't
fritter away the seconds like a spendthrift. Savour them,

they're precious. Life tastes good. And please, my dearest.

"Above all, make sure you don't suffer!"

Suffering is despicable and completely worthless. Just look what a mess it's got me into, this coffin, this casket.

When they die, people become figments of the imagination. You've turned me into a fake creature, like those plastic flowers defiling gravestones, dumped there by philistines in memory of their lovers. I can't even love you because love needs so much strength and generosity – and that's where the living often fall short, those with neither the power nor the heart to love. And then there's us. Me, little more than a crumbling heap of sentences. Words are as tender as metal. You can't kiss someone with a whack from an iron bar.

"Are we playing? Are we still playing?"

Right then: so we're still pretending death is like a school playground where the kids are absorbed in a game of coming-back-to-life. They're certainly experts in killing, and brilliant at war. They don't have much faith in this resurrection lark, but they're willing to have a go, and do end up believing nonetheless. You're entitled to play and pretend you're a believer too. Dress up as a wizard and tap the lift door with your magic wand. It splits in half, opening like Ali Baba's cave.

"Peek-a-boo! Can you see me?"

I'm here. I seem full of life, flush with youth.

"No, don't touch me."

My flesh is all gone, and mirages never turn into real people. They might, at most, worm their way into our homes like superstitions. To leave this letter on your bedside table.

"Now then, off to bed with you!"

Take off your costume, put on your pyjamas. And would you please stick that wand back in your pencil pot!

Dear Charlotte,

January was very short, as if it had some days missing. There were too many to begin with. You wished the month could have broken into a sprint, vaulting over the weeks like hurdles. When you awoke, your tears from the night before still hadn't dried up. The morning walloped you with a headbutt and the afternoon gave you a good kick in the stomach. You spent your evenings doubled over in pain, with a bloodstained face that no amount of crying could wash clean.

There was no blood on your face, but the edges of your eyes were like two red slashes. You got into the habit of putting on make-up, concealing them with kohl, and caking your bruised cheeks with rouge. You did this with painstaking care, as though learning to write. You still hadn't dabbled with those colours, those layers of plaster. Even as a little girl, you'd never felt the need to pinch your mother's lipstick and draw yourself a mouth fit for a woman. Adulthood seemed so far away, and in truth you had no urge to grow up. Now you felt you were painting yourself as someone else, grafting another face onto your own, cobbling together a carnival mask to hide behind.

One day you finally turned yourself in at a hospital. The pain was too intense, and had become more unbearable than the humiliation of handing your brain over to the psychiatrists. You arrived in casualty and said *take it*. Like an infant you might have left with social services, because you lived in dire poverty and wanted the child to survive. You were fearful of dying, of killing yourself. You knew there was a contract out on you, and that you were the one charged with carrying out the deed. Suicide is a form of homicide like any other. A premeditated murder, a plot dreamt up by a cabal in some dark recess of the psyche. A faction that gradually inspires others to join the cause, right up to the night of the revolution.

"I'm in casualty on Avenue Parmentier."

"I'll come and see you tomorrow."

I called you again two days later.

"They let me out."

You'd left hospital with your brain ticking away in your skull, like a time bomb the medical profession felt they needn't bother to defuse. The city was menacing and the buildings were flies, watching your every move through multi-windowed eyes. Cars swept around in herds, determined to trample you underfoot. Passers-by cared nothing for you, and sunlight cut through your image with the slash of a sword.

You went past where I lived but you didn't come up. You

got into a bus that seemed less unpleasant than the others. Sitting alone on the back seat, you closed your eyes for fear of glimpsing your reflection in the empty corridor. You must have mistaken it for a mirror.

Your parents knew nothing of your little trip to the loony bin. When you arrived they were in the middle of lunch. You went to fetch a plate from the kitchen. You had two extra helpings of *blanquette* and polished off every last crumb of bread.

You went away to vomit. You came back looking even sadder than before, wearing the smile of an actress who's too lousy at her craft to be convincing. You began to talk, explaining you'd made the most of a period of sick leave to spend three days with me in a little hotel on the harbour at Saint-Malo.

"We had winkles to eat."

You put your grey coat back on, and the beige scarf I'd given you one day because I'd had it around my neck and you'd thought it was lovely. You left the front door wide open as you disappeared.

The city had changed colour. The sun was hidden behind a dark curtain of clouds. The streetlamps were still off but there was a sense of gathering darkness. Cars had their lights on, and apartment blocks gradually lit up their windows one by one. Pedestrians were walking faster and faster, rushing to throw themselves into the gaping jaws of the metro. You were afraid the entire *arrondissement* would take to the air, flipping on top of you like a casserole dish and burying you under its stones, tarmac, vehicles and people.

You dreaded suicide. You thought dying had to be unpleasant and might even hurt. Yet you wished you'd already been dead for a long time. After a life packed with achievements, in which you'd journeyed through those obligatory decades filled with their share of births and bereavements, of suffering overcome with courage, simple little pleasures like Saturday mornings spent under the duvet, and other essentials which, in your eyes, would have justified your brief stay with us. Quite simply, you wished you'd crossed the finish line with dignity, having run the race with honour. Just as passengers on the eve of a long flight to Asia would prefer to have already landed.

You hadn't been in touch with the skipper for a week. You'd left the ship in the dead of night. He hadn't woken up, and the lapping of the waves had masked the sound of your footsteps on the hull. You were now afraid he'd already set sail, charting a course across the Atlantic, or sailing back up the Rhine among the steamships and barges before flowing into the North Sea along with the river. You suddenly needed him, the way someone who's cold needs warm clothes.

You were running. You didn't bump into anyone; the crowd parted as you got near, like the sea letting the Children of Israel pass through during the Exodus. Panic is frightening, and sends people flying in all directions. Panic carried you forward and you didn't even stop to catch your breath. You crossed Place de la Bastille to the sound of beeping cars, went down Boulevard Henri-IV and passed the Pont de Sully before arriving at Quai de Béthune.

The evening you ran away you remembered seeing Notre-Dame through the porthole. The cathedral hadn't moved an inch, but the boat wasn't moored anywhere in sight. You took a tablet from a box of tranquilisers a nurse had given you to keep you going before throwing you out. You felt less anxious; you were sitting on the trunk of a tree that had just been felled. You were staring at Notre-Dame as it faded to a blur.

I had just finished writing a story. Perhaps it was a tale about love, something I'm not completely unfamiliar with, after all. I'd seen on the Mac that it was almost five in the morning. You called me.

"I'm outside your door."

"Come on up."

"I'm here."

You were on the landing, fingers numb with cold after spending all night on the riverbank. As the drowsiness wore off you tried to make out a white sail on the Seine. Everything was grey, and the noise from the night traffic made a dull echo like tinnitus in your ears.

You went to lie down and slept through until early afternoon.

I heard you running the water in the bathroom. I got up from my desk to make you some coffee. You joined me by the coffee maker. You apologised for arriving unannounced, your voice hoarse because of a cold.

"You might have had company."

"I was expecting you."

"Liar."

You smiled. You reminded me of a bird that's lost some feathers in a storm, and fallen off a branch because so many are missing it can't fly any more. I made you eat a bowl of cereal with milk. You told me about your night. I suggested you call the skipper.

"Instead of standing vigil on the quayside like a sailor's wife."

Your brain hadn't paused to consider this as it fled.

The skipper answered on the first ring. He had taken refuge high up in Montmartre. He'd had a brush with the police because his trimaran had been getting in the way of the tour buses; some tourists were starting to pound it with cameras that were now obsolete, thanks to the new digital revolution which had broken out two days earlier in Taiwan. He was about to hoist the jib and make his way down to Pigalle at low speed. He arranged to meet you at twilight outside a cheesemonger's shop on Rue des Martyrs.

"See you soon."

You kissed me from a distance with a smack of your lips, before vanishing like a niece who abandons her kind-hearted old uncle and whirls out of sight the moment her fiancé gives in and rings her phone after sulking for a whole week.

You returned to work the following Monday. The editor-in-chief asked you to convert to the missionary position, instead of indulging in acrobatics that were so dangerous for your spinal column.

"We're not going to support your sex life with periods of sick leave for much longer."

The radio station was now obsessed with happiness. In future your mission would consist of tracking it through streets, stations and supermarket aisles. When the prison had granted the necessary permissions, it would be your job to flush it out of cells, punishment blocks and high-security areas. One of your colleagues was currently recording its presence deep within the throats of patients nearing the end of their lives. Meanwhile, a young trainee hoped to glean a few snorts of laughter from the very heart of some Périgord truffles; they were drunk with joy at the thought of being sliced up by a majestic knife on a chef's chopping board at the Plaza Athénée.

The editor-in-chief criticised you in passing for hardly looking the part.

"You might at least try smiling; you catch more flies with honey than vinegar."

All week long you'd been trying to store up the happiness of the public in the bowels of your tape recorder. You would poke your mike into a crowd, like the nozzle of a vacuum cleaner into some dusty nook or cranny. You harvested laughs, fond memories of motherhood and drinking binges, and a few growls from grumpy old grouches. This was no miraculous catch of fish, but at least you brought back enough to prepare a little fricassee for them to broadcast, given the noticeable absence of either poached salmon or sea bass with fennel.

When night fell you left on a cruise. The trade winds carried the boat towards the Balearic Islands and the Canaries. One minute you'd be drinking coconut milk in Cape Verde, the next falling asleep in the arms of the skipper within musket range of a red sandy beach in Equatorial Guinea.

At eight in the morning you awoke with a start on the Saint-Martin canal between two rows of tents crammed with homeless people. They were suffering from hypothermia, and opened their eyes to find themselves staring down the lenses of television cameras from across Europe and the Arab world. You knew they viewed happiness as some kind of dodgy food that the well-to-do stuffed down their throats, and you dashed off to catch your metro on Place de la République with your mike clutched firmly in your hands to stop it exploding in their midst, like an insult dangling at the end of a baby-pink cable, as pink as the smiling lips of a teenager who'd just been picked by the radio station as its symbol following its latest cultural revolution.

February had just put in an appearance. An icy corridor leading into the coldest, darkest and shortest March of your life.

You called one evening to say you didn't give a damn

whether you were dead or alive. How much time you had left didn't matter any more, and you would have welcomed cancer with open arms. A brief struggle with pain, the courage to face up to the chemo, and the satisfaction of walking off the set like a diva to wild applause from everyone watching the thirty-fifth episode of your saga as it was disrupted in the middle of filming.

We exchanged a flurry of emails. You asked me to put on an excessive amount of weight so I could carry you in my belly. Unable to give birth, I'd be forced to keep you safe inside me, sheltered from disaster.

"I can't take any more, my life feels like toilet paper, and I'm at the end of the roll."

You asked me to hide you. To hold you captive. To chain you up in a corner. You were as terrified of freedom as of falling from a height.

You'd invite yourself round, very cautiously. As if you dreaded being turned down.

"We could have dinner at your place, I'll bring cakes and daisies."

But perhaps because you were afraid I'd lose interest – or perhaps as a tactical move to make the offer more attractive – you would always suggest a date some way off.

"In a week's time, I can't make it before."

In the meantime you'd drop by out of the blue. Panic-stricken, you'd join me in the warmth of the bed. You were a refugee; the outside world was a war zone. The duvet was like an air-raid shelter, a radiation-proof bunker, or an old shed whose roof is riddled with rusty holes, the kind one's so relieved to find in a clearing during a snowstorm. You'd say *if you want we can make love.*

You'd fall asleep in my arms. You were a lost child.

My poor darling,

So you've turned into a needlewoman, have you? A seam-stress paid by the day? Embroidering, scalloping, embellishing? Are you sewing me a dress, a long dress, a wedding dress with a never-ending train? Are you planning an *haute couture* death for me? And there I was, always getting my stuff in the sales! Condemned women are never dressed that elegantly on the day of their execution: a rough linen nightshirt does the job, and they walk in bare feet. You're pussyfooting around, my dear, dithering along the way, flailing madly to drag out my final moments. You big baby, do you really think time can be spun like sugar?

"Be brave, my boy!"
The gallows have been erected on Place de Grève. Curious crowds have been jostling around since first light; old women, muffled against the cold, are selling mulled wine, marzipan cakes and bacon grilled on open braziers, making the air so smoky that even the dogs are sneezing.
"Look!"
The balconies have all been rented out to piddly little

marquesses, dowagers with glistening lips, and fake count-
esses laughing and sipping champagne, playfully flicking
away a few bubbles that float through the air before
bursting onto the rabble.

There comes a time when the vixen has had enough of the
chase and lets the hounds catch her. She's exhausted, believe
me: she's been on the run for so long, and for her death
brings relief. Carry on making things up, and March will
grow as long as Pinocchio's nose. Go on then, show me
what you're really made of, and let's get to that wretched
moment when a suicidal woman hangs herself. Don't be
like those bald idiots waiting feverishly for spring so their
hair might sprout again along with the grass in the meadow.
You probably assumed I'd come back to life after a harsh
winter of writing, and that, after endless discussions, death
would agree to set me free like a convict at the end of his
sentence?

"Stop forcing me to speak!"
The dead can't be ridiculed like this. You tog me up in
words, making me a floppy hat from adjectives and a
bodice out of adverbs. I'm like a poodle dolled up by her
lustful master in an evening dress, strings of rhinestones and
high-heeled shoes that make her stumble with every step.
He's an old fool who's anxious to launch his creature into
high society, and dreams she'll be invited to the debutante's
ball like any other young virgin.

Now, my friend, allow me to stop this chatter, seal up my letter and fling it into the nothingness that handles our mail so well.

Dear Charlotte,

You were suffering, and life was weighing you down. You told me your skeleton was turning into stone. Moments of happiness were few and far between, yet this made them seem all the more intense. In darkness even the faintest glimmer of light can be dazzling. But you weren't exactly deprived of an orgasm or two, deep in the skipper's arms. Occasionally, on a Sunday morning, you were pleased to see the sun. You'd still listen to music loud enough to blow the cabin to bits, and some evenings the trimaran forced its way through crowds in packed concert halls to let you hear the samba played at top volume.

At the beginning of March the skipper bought you a clarinet at a flea market. You'd dug out the score for Mozart's Concerto in A Minor from the bottom of a box; but by then you only had a couple of weeks left, and you didn't have time to play the whole thing. The priest played the first movement at the end of your funeral mass. It was too long, it dragged on forever, and he had to cut it short so the undertakers could whisk your coffin off to the grave-yard before nightfall.

In time, one stops feeling the pain. Even your job at the radio station no longer upset you. You asked around for details of where happy people lived. You climbed to sixth-floor flats in your search, filling your lungs with joy: straight from the mouths of old idiots, young people pumping drugs into their veins as you watched, or the totally senile, chuckling away with a mad glint in their eyes, who often mistook the furry cover on your mike for a bib. You cleared out your tape recorder hourly in an internet café, like a hunter unloading his kill. When the editor-in-chief was snowed under, your unedited reports streamed straight onto the airwaves.

In the evenings you would sob uncontrollably. The skipper was fed up bailing out your tears. He refused to listen to you any more and abandoned the boat, preferring to sleep in a dry bed belonging to a girl in a happier frame of mind. He didn't reply to your messages, and when he returned, his hair streaked white by the kapok from his conquests' pillows, he threw you overboard. You didn't even feel like standing up; you crawled along the quayside, going back up the boulevards using your arms like the legs of a tortoise; you felt blind and deaf, and sheer instinct steered your carcass forwards, avoiding obstacles at the very last minute, crossing streets by dodging around crazy motorbikes and cars wild with rage; you branched off at junctions, creeping up little alleys and passageways, so your path remained as straight as an arrow, like a line drawn with a ruler on a map of Paris.

That morning I was smoking a cigarette on the terrace

before going to bed. I saw you going past. It was hard to see your face clearly, but I recognised you from your grey coat. You didn't stop. You didn't even bother turning your head towards the building. You continued on your way, getting as far as Rue de Bagnolet.

When you reached Rue Meursault you sat up jerkily and got to your feet again. Your key hadn't rolled out, despite your pocket being torn. You opened the door. You probably bumped into something as you went inside, because you knocked over the copper cauldron where umbrellas were left to dry. Your father came downstairs, thinking you were a burglar. Your coat was tattered and torn, as though you were actually a grey cuddly toy whose fur hadn't survived a mangling from a hyperactive child. Your father said nothing, but you spoke to him all the same.

"The skipper's chucked me out."

He reached for your hand.

"I'm shattered."

You shut yourself away in the studio. He beat on the door with his fist. He took too long to break it open. When he got inside you were dead.

My poor darling,

I've never crept along the ground in my life! I've never been one of those women who spend their lives crawling about on their bellies like reptiles. When will you stop smearing my name with dirt? You didn't love me enough when I was alive – so every time you drag me through the mud, don't expect me to live with the shame or wash myself clean without so much as a whimper. Especially since we need a lantern here to find the launderettes.

I really do regret not having jaw muscles any more, and that I can't take a bite out of you. I ought to send a little gremlin to gouge a hole in your flesh. Or an angel flanked by a neurologist to strip out your brain for a whole weekend. You don't deserve your neurons. Your head is an alchemist's crucible in which your imagination cooks me up like a fantasy. Before I left, I should have made you promise you'd never try and bang me up in one of your books.

"And don't go thinking I'm as thick as two short planks!"

I know full well you wouldn't have kept your word. For peace of mind I ought to have taken you with me. At your age, though, I could hardly leave you in the care of a babysitter. Some hapless sixth-form failure, forever repeating the year, still spotty at twenty-seven, that you'd have screwed on the very first evening when she gave you a bath. You big grizzly baby with your Mont-Blanc instead of a willy, spitting out ink day and night! You're using paper like nappies so you might as well have your novels printed on them too!

My darling, if you weren't a writer, you'd be no worse than anyone else. But you're an obsessive old so-and-so and you'll never have the will to stop.

"So go on then!"

Let's see you climax: ejaculate your prose, make the most of my hanging, what a stroke of luck. Recycle my misfortune, you cruel ecologist, don't let a drop of suffering go to waste. But please, I implore you, never turn me into a tortoise again. I stayed on two feet to the bitter end.

"You too, stand up straight!"

Don't hunch your shoulders! Tell the tale of my death as if it were a battle; a battle one loses, true, but then death always ends in defeat.

Off you go, sleep well, little scribe. And try to forget me from time to time, to give yourself a break. You were so good at forgetting me before I hanged myself.

Dear Charlotte,

On 20 March 2007 you were up at a quarter to eight. You took a shower, and dressed in blue cords and a turtleneck sweater you went upstairs to join your parents. You had a cup of coffee with them. It was cold, and your mother complained about the boiler that had a mind of its own, grinding to a halt in the middle of the night only to fire up again at daybreak.

You'd seen the skipper the day before. He'd made the effort to spend part of the evening trying to console you. Around ten, he climbed back up to the bridge to check on the moorings. You'd caught him standing against the mast where, despite a biting wind, he was clinging to a girl who'd unzipped her parka. You'd decided to come back here and sleep alone.

"Have a good day, you guys."

"Don't forget, we're having dinner with you tomorrow evening."

A meal to celebrate twenty-five years of marriage.

"I'm thinking of nothing else."

You left them with a smile on your face which they remembered later.

The air in the street felt less bracing than inside the house. You found a place to sit in the metro. You laid my latest book on your knees; you'd been lugging it around in your bag for several weeks. Even though you resented it for being as heavy as a sack of spuds. You opened it at random, but you'd already read this tale of passion fizzling out, in which the protagonists agree to stay together against the odds so as not to inflict the pain of breaking up on each other.

There was a new girl behind reception at the radio station. The editor-in-chief was away; it was rumoured she'd gone for a mammogram, but no-one knew if this was true.

"So she's forty, that's ancient."

A journalist from a fashion magazine was being interviewed live on air. According to her, happiness was all the rage this spring.

"Perhaps even more so than teeth whitening and foalskin mules."

You were in a good mood, practically chuckling. You headed off to collect your tape recorder, like cops picking up their firearms in the morning.

It was turning colder, and as you went out you noticed a few snowflakes falling from the sky. You didn't feel up to facing the corridors of the metro again, and so you walked as far as Place de l'Opéra.

You took out your mike in front of a merchant bank on

Boulevard des Capucines. The people going in and out weren't exactly overjoyed about the way you extended your hand to beg for a word or two, words they appeared as reluctant to part with as cash. A man with white hair matching the stripes on his jacket shielded himself with his briefcase, afraid you might pinch the odd syllable.

You went to the Café de la Paix. You dipped your mike in an old woman's cup of tea. She began screaming, as if you'd violated some intimate part of her body and made her think she was being indecently assaulted. You fled before the shocked waiters had the presence of mind to call the police.

You reached the Printemps store on Boulevard Haussmann. You were no longer convinced you'd carried out the crime. It seemed more likely that, at the last minute, you hadn't entered the café, fearing you'd be driven away like a crook attempting to steal customers' conversations. You listened to that morning's recordings. You could hear the sound of cups, glasses clinking, and a lady's voice requesting you politely not to take her picture.

"I've got wrinkles, you know."

"They'll only see your voice."

"I don't want to be seen at all."

She was probably afraid some new technology would enable her face to be seen by breaking down the sound frequencies in her voice. You couldn't be bothered annoying her any further.

You lit a cigarette. It tasted wonderful because you'd kept

off them for a whole three days in the firm belief you'd never smoke again. The nicotine intake went straight to your head, as though you'd had a glass of alcohol. The effect of the first puff wore away, plunging you into an intense state of lucidity and panic. Your life was a series of cliffs with jagged outlines and sharp ridges. A frozen, polar landscape. Your future was dazzling, blinding you with light. You were as petrified as a rabbit in a thicket, caught in the glare of a gendarme's torch as he scours the country-side in the dead of the night, searching for a kidnapped child.

You decided to hand in your notice. Your mike had become your bread-and-butter, because you'd been waving it around like bait in trying to ensnare happiness. You despised it as much as gold you'd been made to scrape from the depths of a mine in galleries long since picked clean by generations of convicts. You'd probably glean only tiny, barely tangible specks, drowned like sequins in a sea of mud.

If your parents grew tired of putting you up, you'd savour another slice of life at the women's hostel. When you'd had enough of begging for work from reluctant employers, you might even agree to pursue a career in the Salvation Army in the hope of retiring as a second lieu-tenant.

At midday you sent me a bizarre message, asking if I was prepared to take you on as a bathroom attendant. I replied the following day saying I was ready to offer you the post of sofa technician. You were already dead.

Head down, and with her right hand concealing her mouth, the girl at reception was secretly talking on her mobile. You got into the lift with an ugly-looking man whose skin was almost grey. It seemed like he was wearing a photocopy of his face, saving the original for special occasions. You arrived at the first floor. He pressed the button for the eleventh and disappeared into the upper reaches of the building.

You bumped into the weather girl. She had tears in her eyes because the rotten weather had undermined her credibility: the day before she'd given a rosy forecast out of kindness, trying not to demoralise listeners who were depressed enough as it was by the unemployment figures. You lent her a hanky. You told her you were going to see the boss.

"She's still not back."

She told you they now suspected she'd sunk into the menopause, and at that very moment could be found on a private hospital operating table in the Batignolles, enjoying a consolatory facelift paid for by her husband.

"I'm handing in my notice."

"Well, I'm waiting to be fired and get six months' salary."

"Tell her I'm packing it in."

She shrank back when you held out your tape recorder. You placed it on the floor.

You left, having laid down your arms. You crept down

the stairs, like someone fleeing the scene of a crime without drawing attention before melting into the crowd. The editor-in-chief was getting into the lift just as you emerged into the entrance hall. You recognised her from the long black plait tossed across her shoulder like a scarf. But she had her back to you, and you passed by without being seen.

You sat on the heated terrace of a little café and ordered a salad. You left it untouched and scarcely took a sip of Coke. You jabbed at the buttons on your mobile. The skipper didn't answer. You left him messages that were passionate, offhand, irritated or downright furious. People around you broke off their conversations when you raised your voice.

In the metro you realised you'd left without paying. You got off at Charonne. It was around three in the afternoon. I wasn't at home. You rang my doorbell for ages. That evening, the concierge told me a young woman in a state of anxiety had gone into the lodge to ask whether she'd seen me since the day before.

"He came by in the morning to pick up a registered parcel."

"Thank goodness."

You looked relieved. Admittedly, a few weeks earlier I'd shown symptoms of a heart attack that turned out to be a false alarm. Perhaps you were afraid they'd got the diagnosis wrong, and the beast had in fact died suddenly, its claws still hooked around the letters on the keyboard. Or maybe you didn't rate my chances of clinging onto life that highly, and imagined me lying in the kitchen in a pool of blood after a crude attempt at hara-kiri.

You headed down to the basement. The smell of insecticide made you cough. You walked along the corridor between the cellars. They reminded you of dungeons. It seemed as if some of the doors had burst open when prisoners, driven insane through solitary confinement, had rammed them with their heads. You made your way through the car park. You got lost in a maze of dirty concrete. The vehicles were lined up like wine barrels in a vault.

You found mine, with four wheels like the others, but badly dented and with its back smashed in; it was barely a teenager, having the previous summer celebrated the twelfth anniversary of leaving the factory. You knew I no longer locked the doors, to let dishonest people pinch my dashboard without breaking the windows. You sat in the driver's seat and extended it fully. You pretended to fall asleep, but couldn't convince yourself you were sleeping.

You dialled the skipper's number. You couldn't get a signal. You turned the phone over, stretched out your arm and took a photo. Your parents discovered it after you died, stored in the device's memory. A shadowy face, a dark head against a black background; and yet one that remained clearly identifiable from its shape, as though cut out with great care. Perhaps you'd taken this mysterious photo by accident, during a sudden, involuntary movement caused by an attack of nerves. Your parents deleted it, preferring to hold onto memories of you infused with light and colour.

A man renting a two-room apartment on the ground floor caught sight of you when he came to fetch his brand-new Peugeot; he cherished it even more than the motorcyclist's heart he'd received as a transplant the year before at the Boucicaut Hospital. He suspected you were the protagonist in a real-life crime drama. After taunting him with a Stanley knife, you were going to make your escape at the wheel of his car, leaving him behind in a pool of blood and guts with his belly slit open. He bent over double, and walking on tiptoe like a primate trying not to be noticed, left the car park via the door to the rubbish store that happened to be just behind him.

He hopped up the stairs. He asked the concierge to call the police. She refused, because he'd already caused utter pandemonium a week earlier by mistaking a pile of boxes at the back of the bike shed for the shadow of a prowler.

"I'll take a look anyway."

He didn't want to go with her. And she went into the basement to solve this new mystery.

She came back upstairs with you. She thought you seemed off-colour. She couldn't see why you'd felt compelled to take shelter in my car.

"I'm going to call a doctor."

"I'm not sick."

"You look out of sorts."

She offered you a cup of coffee in the lodge. You asked her whether she'd seen me going past shortly before.

"No."

"Do you think he'll be back soon?"

"I've no idea."

"Does he sleep here every night?"

"I don't know."

"Hasn't he mentioned a trip, or a book signing abroad, or a ski holiday?"

"To be honest, he doesn't talk to me very much."

You peered intently at the large window behind her. Now and again someone would pass by. A wheezy old man, or an overexcited young woman dragging a little boy throwing a tantrum.

"Do you think it's getting dark?"

"Oh no, not yet."

She lifted the curtain on a different window, a little one that gave onto the grassy inner courtyard.

"It's not sunny any more."

"We haven't seen the sun since Monday."

She poured you another cup of coffee. You knocked it back in one gulp. Tears welled up in your eyes.

"Do you feel ill?"

"I've burnt myself."

"Would you like a glass of water?"

"I hope they've not taken him to hospital."

"Why?"

You were thinking of two people at the same time. As you spoke you were sending text messages that piled up in the skipper's inbox. You got to your feet.

"Perhaps he came back without you noticing."

"Just give him a ring."

"Thanks for the coffee."

You left the lodge. You huddled in a corner of the hallway. You remained on the lookout. When you spied the concierge disappearing down the narrow corridor that led to her quarters, you made a dash for the lifts without being spotted.

Concerned at hearing you ring the bell for so long, and so often, my neighbour across the landing popped out of his burrow. He looked you up and down in silence, before concluding you were probably some spurned mistress who'd decided to rekindle the relationship at any price. He went back to hanging up his washing.

His machine had never been good at spin-drying, but far from mending its ways, it had been making a complete hash of the job for some time. The washing would emerge dripping from the drum, and he had to wring it out in the bathtub like a washerwoman before spreading it on the clothes horse.

Once the chore was done he poured himself a whisky. He drank it standing up with his coat on, because he had to report for duty at six in a brasserie on Place de la République where he'd be serving drinks until morning.

As he left, he saw you stretched out lifeless on the ground. Your head was on the doormat, and your eyes and forehead were hidden by a tuft of hair. It didn't occur to him that, having waited so long, you had gradually sunk into a heap and dozed off. He could already see himself being summoned to the police station to make a statement, explaining the circumstances in which he'd discovered your body.

The concierge's services were needed once more and she arrived on the scene a few minutes later. She repeated the words *mademoiselle, mademoiselle* in your ear, and you gradually came round. You yawned as you stretched. To this day she's convinced she then saw you smile. Whatever the case, you never smiled at anyone again, right up to the moment you hanged yourself.

You came downstairs with her. You told her you'd finally come back to life after years of suffering that were just like a long illness. You were now beginning your convalescence.

"I feel light."

And strangely liberated too.

"I'm so happy, it does you good, being born."

In the entrance hall you wished her a good evening. You even turned back to say how much you liked her hair colour.

"I've always loved strawberry blond."

"People tend to say it's light brown."

You remained standing in front of her in the hall. You hoped she'd reply and invite you into the lodge for another natter.

"I need to put the bins out."

Your mouth twisted itself into a miserable excuse for a smile, if it could even be called that. A trace of a scowl that hadn't managed to break free of its chrysalis; the concierge would later speak of a frozen grin.

"And I need to go to the hairdresser."

You left.

The snow had returned as darkness fell. You crossed the street. You went into a hairdressing salon, one you'd often gone past but never set foot in until then. Apparently a customer had just made a last-minute cancellation.

"You're in luck."

You went off with hair as red as an autumn leaf. Cut into a bob, as though framing your face, ready for display in the shop window of a dealer in paintings or antiques, or one of those photographers born in the first half of the last century who still cultivate the art of portraiture at the back of their premises.

You arrived in Rue Meursault at seven-thirty. You'd bought a bottle of vodka on the way, which you put in the studio's cute little fridge. You would share it that night with the skipper. You had won back your freedom and would sprinkle it generously over the trimaran as it set sail for points unknown; at daybreak you'd discover a turquoise bay, where you would spend twenty or thirty years on holiday before settling as a couple of young pensioners in Paris. A city that had improved no end over time, transformed into a leisure resort where people could sample pure happiness, like taking the waters in a spa. A mawkish, hideous dream, enough to merit jumping from the top of the Montparnasse Tower.

You went upstairs. You turned on the table lamp. Its feeble glow infused the room with dim light, like a bedroom. You lay down on the sofa. There were some cold ashes in the fireplace, relics from the weekend before. You hadn't put your mobile back in its case. Your messages were probably beginning to clog up the server's memory. It would soon be full to the brim, and a battalion of engineers would be dispatched to clear it out before infuriated customers decided to take their business elsewhere.

You'd have liked to send the skipper something other than language, other than screams. To send him tears, kisses and even yourself in bite-sized chunks, yourself in your entirety, bit by bit. You'd have re-assembled yourself piece by piece, like a jigsaw, and you'd have leapt into his arms when he accessed his voicemail. You did not love him any more, but your love for him lived on deep within you like a reflex.

You listened to his greeting. You pictured him sealed inside a glass cubby-hole, tirelessly repeating after each bleep that he'd call back as soon as possible, like an electrical store's recorded after-sales message.

You switched on the television. It was the last advert before the news, for a brand of denture fixative. You thought about me because I might have false teeth one day, even if you still hadn't celebrated your fifty-fifth birthday. By now your concern for me had faded away; every last trace was gone.

Your dogged determination in trying to contact the skipper became automatic. You didn't bother actually speaking; instead, you'd hold out the phone facing the TV, sending him news about Iraq or some tennis player who'd breached her suspension order, lapsed into drug abuse and become yesterday's news.

You closed your eyes. You were imprisoned behind eyelids as heavy as lead. You were back in a war zone, where the enemy's tanks were demolishing the flimsy battlements you'd taken years to construct. Your army was in retreat, and though many troops were still locked in battle, entire squadrons had already made good their escape. Exhaustion had made cowards of your soldiers. You needed courage to open your eyes again, but you'd have needed even more to keep them shut.

The adverts were back. A film started. But the words weren't coming out of the actors' mouths. A man hidden behind the screen was whispering them through a straw. As a child, you knew perfectly well that whole tribes of people were encamped within the buttresses of the television's outer shell. They would bide their time before putting in an appearance, sometimes so veiled in secrecy there was barely time to spot them, let alone remember what they looked like. When it was time for the news, a man wearing a tie would clench his teeth behind a desk, lips curled back in readiness. His legs were nowhere to be seen: either they'd been cut off, or he'd never had any in the first place. He was terrified he'd soon have to join his fellow creatures in the darkness of the plastic box, where they lived cheek by jowl in the most cramped conditions imaginable.

Nowadays, advances in technology had made these characters redundant. The only one left was this guy with his straw. He was still living somewhere in the house, lurking undercover like an outlaw. He would pop up whenever the sound disappeared. The sentences he whispered traced a curve in the air before falling back down to slip inside your ears.

When you turned off the telly he returned to his hiding place. You could barely hear him as he gasped for breath, like an actor who's just come off stage after an endless monologue. You went over to the fireplace. You held your hands above the hearth, as though the ashes might turn back into glowing embers to console you. You could feel an intense heat; perhaps the ashes had retained their memory of the fire. Unless the conflict blazing through your brain was making you feverish. Your hands were clammy, your forehead was burning and your lips quivered slightly.

You went into the kitchen. On the table a pineapple was lying on its side, like a head that had fallen asleep wearing a ludicrous green hat. You took two sachets of aspirin from the large drawer where, sooner or later, all the medicines in the house tended to wash up, like flotsam and jetsam. You diluted them and drank the mixture. You sat down on one of the lemon-yellow Formica chairs bought the year before at the bric-a-brac sale on Rue Léon-Frot.

You had a sudden desire to throw every bit of food in the kitchen into a bucket. To liquidise it in the blender and drink the nourishing mush until you collapsed on the tiles intoxicated with grub, having eaten the meal to end all meals. If by chance you came back to life, you'd empty your stomach, now as massive as the globe, down the bottomless pit of the toilet.

The world surrounded you. But you weren't on top,

placed on the surface of the planet. You were deep inside: a woman, a little girl, a human petal torn from the rest of its kind, no longer attached to its flower, no longer attached to anything at all, lost in the middle of a whirlwind of cities, greenery, the blue of the sea, the past, with ruined monuments, the fossilised bones of species swallowed by the sands of time, and the maelstrom of the future, that tragedy just waiting to happen.

You blinked your eyes as little as possible, for fear they'd seize the chance never to open again. You were trying to remain on the fringes of this conflict, to be little more than your outermost skin. A layer that grew thinner and thinner, a film of consciousness, pearls of dew that would appear like sweat on your forehead.

You were going to chuck out your brain, like an old sponge soaked in used oil, all black and reeking of anguish that could easily clog up the local drains. Perhaps you'd wring it out before getting rid of it, but not one drop would fall in the sink; and when you tried rinsing it in running water, it would act all pig-headed and refuse to be cleaned, like a bad-tempered child recoiling when faced with the shower.

Even madness didn't scare you any more; lunacy would have allowed you to fly off, to exchange your former hell for a new one, to feel you were running away by slipping from one misery to another. Moving on is exhilarating, because no matter how gloomy the sky remains, one sees it from a different corner of the street; and if one happened to leap into the unknown of an evening, it would be from another window.

Your mobile rang. A colleague was calling you from Orly. She was boarding a flight to Sudan in ten minutes. There just had to be people there who were happy to be alive despite famine and war. Contrary to all expectations, she'd approached the management on your behalf and had won you a pardon. From your act of rebellion that morning.

"The resignation letter you gave Mélanie in the corridor."

Your punishment would be no more than an official warning together with a fourteen-day suspension. You'd receive a registered letter by the end of the week.

"Make the most of it and take a holiday."

She'd seen some amazing bargains on lastminute.com. You could go off and lie in the Caribbean sun for the price of three pairs of shoes and a dishwasher on special offer.

"I'm going to have to change my old one."

You didn't say anything, you weren't listening. You were holding the phone with both hands, staring at it. Her voice drifted out like smoke rings, signals from a tribe whose language you no longer understood. You were probably being given news from a faraway village you'd never set foot in again. People from your past lingered on there: muttering, dancing, crying in unison with the sky on rainy days and trying to please each other, as if they needed to feel as desirable as a strawberry tart in a patisserie window just to have the strength to keep going.

"I might as well get some fags at the duty free."

Boarding was delayed. She kept you on the line; you could hear her hurrying towards the shop.

"They don't have any menthol cigarettes left."

She was drawn to a powder compact.

"Mine's empty, and there's no way I'll find one in Sudan."

The Chivas Regal was tempting but alcohol was prohibited there.

"That's enough to get me stoned to death, like the last of the filthy sluts."

But some chocolate would do nicely.

"The in-flight meals are always disgusting."

Some spare deodorant.

"You'd sweat to death in Sudan."

Some eau de parfum.

"If the streets really stink, I'll shove a bit on a hanky and hold it to my nose."

She remembered her skin peeling the previous summer.

"All over my neck and shoulders."

She put a tube of sunblock in her basket. She asked whether you knew a good dermatologist.

"Mine's a tetraplegic."

The result of a road accident.

"The girl was short-sighted, they should never have given her a licence."

You stared at your fingers resting on the table. You put your face right up close. You laid your forehead on top. You let your head drop. You left it there, on the table, in the same position as the pineapple. The mobile fell to the floor.

"What's that noise? Are you cooking?"

She'd be back on Wednesday. Her voice couldn't travel far enough for you to hear. In any case, you were no longer sure what day it was.

"We could go for lunch when you're back from holiday."

You were lucky, going to laze around in the Caribbean for a whole week. She probably wouldn't have time to go swimming in Khartoum. Besides, the Red Sea had always frightened her.

"You'd be as well doing the breaststroke in a blood-bath."

She wasn't the kind to go bathing in blood, like the coquettes of ancient Rome. She chuckled. Her laughter bubbled up from the mobile like a tiny fountain, and splashed down like rain on the terracotta tiles.

"I don't know what I've done with my boarding card."

She found it all crumpled up in her compact.

"That's very odd, really."

It must have flipped open in the depths of her bag and snapped its jaws around the card after a sudden jolt.

"I think they're calling me."

She ran to the desk.

"Lots of love, darling, and make sure you get plenty of rest."

She hung up and dived into the tunnel that led to Khartoum.

You heard the front door opening. You emerged from your torpor. Your parents were back. They'd been for dinner at a friend's house, someone you'd heard endless talk about, ever since he'd won enough on the lottery to buy a hamlet in the Ardèche and a house on Rue Croulebarbe.

They were in good spirits, chatting loudly, like young people who'd perhaps had a few beers. You remembered that, one evening when you were little, you and your sister had painted the living room orange while your parents were at the cinema. When they discovered the devastation they were ready to skin you alive, like a pair of rabbits for the cooking pot. You were given a reprieve at the last minute. You even remembered them coming to kiss you in bed. Since then you had always preferred living in rooms whose walls were scratched and cracked, or riddled with cuts and bruises, but still spotlessly clean (because they'd been washed so often), rather than go anywhere near a paint-brush.

Your parents gave you a shout when they saw the light in the living room. You didn't answer. They went into the kitchen. Your back was as straight as a ruler, your head stock-still on top of your neck like a lampshade. Your mother said later you'd gone a strange white colour, and your father said you had the glazed look of those artificial eyeballs they put in people with only one eye.

"I've split up with him."

You bent down to pick up your mobile.

"He's cheating on me."

You didn't have the generosity of spirit to think about the nights you'd recently spent in my bed. You no longer had a grain of generosity left; in fact, you didn't have much that was yours at all. You were no more than a tiny wisp of your former self: war had stripped you bare, leaving you a cramped little space to live in, an enclosure whose fences would shatter in a violent attack by enemy troops.

"I'm going to bed."

You gave the pineapple a slap and it began to roll, coming to a halt at the edge of the table.

"I'm not hungry."

You left the room. You walked quickly, crossing the living room like a street in a downpour. You were going to leap to the bottom of the stairs in a single bound, as though it only had one step. But, unexpectedly, you came down slowly, grasping the worn-out rope that did for a banister.

You closed the studio door gently behind you, although there was no risk of a child inside being robbed of his sleep.

You lay down in the darkness. The light from your mobile lit your face. You sent some text messages. They sneaked across Paris. Not like those booming distress flares launched by shipwrecked sailors. The skipper had set the tiller to automatic pilot. He was sleeping alone in the cabin. The trimaran had sailed across the North Sea, gone past Norway, and on arrival at the Pole had plunged into space. It was now revolving around the Earth; but the ceiling, the roof, the clouds and the glare from the city all stopped you from catching sight of its sails. Your messages went astray before reaching the stratosphere and ended up plummeting into the ocean, the eternal snows of the Andean Cordillera, or the middle of a crowded square in São Paulo under the midday sun, where no-one noticed your words vanishing into thin air, the very instant they collided with the scorching tarmac.

Upstairs, your mother was searching for reasons to be hopeful. She imagined you being perked up by a homeopath, a relaxation therapist, or one of those Asian shamans thrusting their sharpened *banderillas* into the meridians of melancholia, stemming the flow of black bile from the mists of time that was poisoning our race. Your father imagined nothing at all. He remained silent.

They went to bed at one in the morning. A gauzy veil of sleep, a cloud of unconsciousness floating above their utter despair. They could see you through it, just as you'd looked in the kitchen, etched straight into the stone that made up your face. Yet they were sure they were sleeping. They recognised sleep from its nightmares.

You'd just applied some lipstick in the dark. You switched on your father's computer. The room was flooded with a bluish light. You had recently begun writing your memoirs. A document of around twenty lines or so, codenamed *Mossy coat*. You were barely at the prologue, at the bit when your biological father got into the bed where your mother lay quaking, waiting for him to come and deposit that little creature from the end of his penis; it would grow in her womb for nine months, and very shortly it would hang itself. You deleted everything with a single click. Then you made the text reappear before closing the file.

You took the bottle of vodka from the fridge. You carried it to the bathroom. You were both reflected in the mirror. The label was the same shade of *scarlet kiss* as your mouth. You'd just decided, yet again, that you weren't going to die. You'd give up drinking, remain clear-headed, keep on the lookout, resist the latest attack and put off your execution. But you might suddenly have a change of heart, smashing your skull against the mirror or the wall, making it shatter like a magnum of champagne swung against a ship's hull at its naming ceremony. You knocked the bottle against the basin. A sliver of glass nicked your cheek. You wiped the blood away with your finger.

Your mother remembers hearing the front door opening and slamming shut twice. She thought you'd gone for a walk, or a run, trying to wear the beast out, forcing your body to fall asleep on your return, and preventing it from becoming an accomplice to murder.

It happened just before seven-thirty. The alarm clock rang upstairs as your mother went into the studio where you were lying on the carpet, your head in your fists, legs bent, warm, eyes closed, peaceful, like a baby who's not yet made the effort to be born.

My poor darling,

People really might think I killed myself just so you'd have
the pleasure of turning the whole affair into a story, one of
those sordid tales you like so much. I was the one that
hanged myself, not you, because you're too much of a
wimp, too much of a coward, and you'd have been too
scared of breaking your neck. Death would have cast a
shadow over the buzz you'd get from talking about your
execution. You'd love to be a martyr, provided you could
brag about it afterwards.

"Funny little fisherman!"

You've got death wriggling at the end of your line, and
you toss it into a book like a fish to the bottom of a net.
You're wearing yourself out, waving it around as you
wander the streets of the Old Port so every last sprog in
Marseille knows you were brave enough to go near it,
brush up against it, the way a kid in the playground boasts
about tickling a girl's pussy. Let's get this over and done
with; don't eke me out any further. Bury me. Let me rest.

As for you.

"Get yourself off to bed!"

And tomorrow, sit back and watch time go by – don't

spend your entire life dreaming of sticky trails of words left in your wake, like the slime left behind by a snail. So make yourself a verbena infusion instead of all this tea, listen to the silence, and try falling silent too.

"You could even forget all about me."

It's not good, thinking about the dead. You should have remembered them before. They, too, only thought of you when they had the memory to do so. Don't forget: in passing away, they've forgotten you forever. They're the ones who started it all, of their own free will, out of frailty, carelessness, old age or sloppiness. They're not worthy of our admiration for having lived, and deserve our contempt for being no more. There's no excuse for being absent. Enjoy the company of those who are still around. People have always needed mouths and stomachs to indulge themselves at a feast. Loving someone has always required a beating heart, and a penis standing to attention, almost throbbing because it's so full of life, so completely the opposite of what we've become in our tombs, our urns and the gardens where our ashes lie scattered.

I'm sealing this letter up just in case, to have a clear conscience. But rumour has it the angels are on holiday, and we've no other postal workers here. They're a sort of carrier pigeon, dropping down your chimneys like Father Christmas. Besides, people like you who live in homes without a hearth can't hope to get any mail at all from our distant lands. If one day you claimed to possess any kind of letter from me franked in the hereafter, I'd know you were bragging, lying and abusing your authority!

I'm sending you a kiss, my darling. Because, in truth, you love yourself enough to kiss yourself all on your own.

Dear Charlotte,

Your father came downstairs wearing a dressing gown with its belt trailing behind. He called the fire brigade. They arrived ten minutes later. Your mother was still holding your body clasped in her arms. They prised it from her. She was asked to leave the room. They set about giving CPR, but were swiftly interrupted by the doctor when he realised the vertebrae had snapped. He viewed your death as suspicious, ticking the box on the death certificate marked *Permission for burial withheld pending forensic examination*. He called the police.

Your parents had sat down on the stairs. Tears streamed down your father's face. Your mother was still living and breathing. She even gave a start when the cops charged into the house. The forensics team came and took some photos and fingerprints. You were carried away on a covered stretcher. Your mother wanted to go with you but she was restrained by a policeman.

The detective went upstairs with your parents. He informed them they were now in police custody. He smoked a cigarette at the window as he waited for them to get dressed. With his left hand he searched through the voicemail messages on your mobile, which he'd found at the foot of the bed. He didn't put your parents in handcuffs. They left Rue Meursault in his official Peugeot 307.

When they arrived at the police station in the 20th *arrondissement* they were separated. They were questioned in adjoining offices for seven hours. The case for homicide was doubtful. As was that for suicide.

The countless text messages you'd sent the skipper during the night focused attention on him. All attempts to contact him had proved futile. His phone had dropped into the sea earlier in the evening while he was tacking off Bolivia. He was finally located between two spy satellites that had confused his trimaran with a UFO. A small group of astronauts, livid at being disturbed while cleaning their space station (which had turned into a real pigsty due to leaving drinks for an intern), parachuted him onto the police station car park around midday.

A surly young policewoman broke the news of your suicide. He managed to keep smiling while she questioned him, in a sort of chipboard cage whose only window looked onto the end of a corridor. He regretted the fact that your actions had endangered his mental well-being.

"But I'll cope."

He was brought face-to-face with your parents, who'd finally been reunited after signing their statements. Before going home, the detective decided the case was closed. All three were released. The skipper suggested to your father they should get to know each other better in a wine bar where you sometimes went for a drink together. Your father didn't reply, but the skipper assumed this meant he wasn't thirsty.

You were now by the river on Quai de la Rapée, tidied away in a drawer of the forensic science laboratory. Ambulances would deliver tramps who'd perished by drowning, suffocated kids, disembowelled grannies, mutilated bodies with pizza-like faces, and even a large fully-dressed monkey which rescuers tackling a fire in a squat had mistaken for a little bearded man. You'd become one of the female passengers aboard this waterside mortuary, seemingly poised to sail off down the Seine like a barge.

Nine whole days passed before you were laid to rest. Your parents visited you every morning. You were moved to another room, as quiet as a bank vault. An employee opened your drawer and they approached without making a sound. They must have been afraid of waking you. They kept you company for a while, as if you were a sick child. Perhaps they were speaking to you in silence, without uttering a word. You were no longer there and yet your body, still intact, was you all the same.

Then they went back to Rue Meursault. The sales rep from the undertakers sat beside them on the sofa. He opened his briefcase, and with an admirable display of professional sorrow offered them a catalogue to choose your coffin. Your sister arrived from England with nothing more than a backpack for luggage. Your grandfather called from Berry with the news he'd just bought a burial plot. The stonemason had promised the gravestone would be ready on the day of the funeral. Your aunt had been to see the local priest, and the mass would take place as planned at two-thirty. She'd booked the village hall so the family could get together after the burial.

"I'll put a picture of her on a table, and a book for everyone to write a few words."

There was a ring at the door. An elated cousin burst into the house carrying lilies. She was disappointed your remains weren't on view in the bedroom. That evening a friend, or perhaps he was a relation, someone nobody knew that well, came to offer prayers and burn incense in the studio.

Your mobile had been given back to your parents. Your father conscientiously dialled all the numbers in your contact list.

"Something terrible's happened, Charlotte's hanged herself."

Occasionally, someone would blame the world of work, childhood memories or the zeitgeist for suffocating you.

"We don't know anything, we have to respect what she did."

He hung up. His composure stemmed from his anger. A dull, unremitting anger, directed at no-one, at death which would never be the victim of a contract killer. He looked your mother in the eye and screamed he was going to top himself too. Your sister left the house in a daze. They brought her back. A doctor was called to give her a sedative.

On Friday 30 March 2007 everyone is up before dawn. Some coffee with bread and butter, gulped down like medicine to cope with the strain. The body begins its final journey from Quai de la Rapée. Despite numerous attempts, the skipper hasn't managed to retrieve his trimaran, lost high in the sky. He sails up and down the Seine in a little boat. He struggles to play a funeral march on the bagpipes. He doesn't dare set foot on land to be near you.

Your mother, who I've never seen before, takes me in her arms. Then she leads me into the cell where you're now lying on a white pad. She holds my hand, squeezing it tight. She utters a sentence I can't remember. But that's when I realise I was a man who mattered in your life. In the coffin there's a woolly sheep, a doll whose pretty face is stained with felt-tip, and some tatty little toys.

"Her sister put them in."

Your sister, who your father is pulling towards him, to make her let go of you and allow the staff to put the lid on. I kiss your lips before the box is closed. The staff take you away. We follow you solemnly into the spacious hallway, our faces drained. Outside, a North African family are waiting for us to clear out of the way and let them mourn their loved one in another room. Your coffin is slid into the hearse. Your father tells me the journey will take some time.

"A hearse can only go so fast."

Your mother thinks I'm in bad shape.

"Don't take your car."

She asks a work colleague to take care of me.

"Look after him, will you."

He leads me away, a hand on my shoulder. He's parked on Boulevard Bourdon. We're on the motorway. The little church is surprisingly packed for a village where no-one appears to live. The people from the radio station have chartered a coach. It seems they've all come, and switched off the transmitter as a mark of respect. The dying words of the mass, the final nail in your coffin. Our procession follows you to the graveyard. Just behind me someone is talking.

"It's a good job it's not raining."

They dump you at the bottom of a hole.

My poor darling,

You've made fast work of burying me. A funeral that's over in a flash, after such a sudden death. There you go, rushing to get this bleak tale done and dusted. But hang on: I remember them devoting a whole day to me, from dawn to dusk. And you dedicated that day to me as well. For someone normally so mean with his time, that's really touching. I'll make the most of this fictional letter to thank you.

You could have brought me a bouquet, or a rose. Even if you hate flowers and think they're vulgar things to offer the dead. You hadn't written one word of a eulogy either, nor paid me the slightest compliment. You might at least have recited a poem, like you did for Mother's Day when you were at school. Clearly, one mustn't ask too much of you.

At the mortuary you screamed and cursed at those who'd never loved me enough. You had a wooden beam in each eye, and three people fell flat on their backs every time you moved your head.

When I'd been laid in my grave, you expressed your gratitude for my life, your face all messy with tears and snot. There were, in your opinion, people who deserved more credit than others for deciding to carry on living each morning. You said I was now safe in God's arms.

"Those tender arms where true bliss is yours."

You must have found this sentence on some fundamentalist website.

Had rigor mortis not prevented my limbs from functioning, I'd have given you a round of applause. My handsome atheist! My Catholic non-believer! My beloved crybaby! Tears flooded down on my coffin, drumming on top like a sudden downpour. It hadn't rained so much in that little graveyard for years.

For eight days the gutters in Rue de Charonne had overflowed with your sobs, and the storm drains were powerless to stop it. A lorry skidded on a puddle of tears, smashed the window of a hairdressing salon and killed the woman who'd cut my hair for the last time.

Your wooden floor had received such a soaking it was starting to rot. You squelched around the living room in old slippers and a bathrobe, like a religious fanatic in a swamp. You called friends, acquaintances, people standing for President, heads of state from the back of beyond whose secretarial staff redirected your calls to dumbfounded press officers, priests, rabbis in central Asia, monks on Patmos and religious figures of all kinds who you woke in the middle of the night, asking them to pray for me.

You didn't exactly leave them much choice. Denying a

few coins to a tramp is one thing; but refusing to pray for the salvation of a desperate woman's soul is quite another. All the prayers you'd demanded of those poor people, paralysed with fear, that you'd ordered to kneel, prostrate themselves, and beg the Lord to spare me from roasting in hell and shorten my passage through purgatory – where, on the pretext of washing my sins away, I would fall victim to the most terrible cruelty, the kind meted out in reform schools from the last century.

You couldn't pray yourself.

"I'm not a believer."

"Why ask for prayers, then?"

"That's a mystery."

A new mystery of faith which you'd just dreamt up and Saint Augustine had never thought of!

"You went out."

Your compass had gone haywire. You went down as far as Bastille, and then headed back north where, slumped on the parapet of a bridge, you watched the cars streaming past on the ring road. You ended your day in the Latin Quarter, searching for the Great Mosque. The imam surely wouldn't refuse you a prayer for the dead; and if there just happened to be an ayatollah close to hand, he'd probably have the Pope's contact details in his address book. He might – after endless negotiations – agree to conduct some kind of service with him, in the name of a new ecumenicalism whose origins lay in my chaotic inner life and my hanging.

You landed up at the Arab World Institute and whirled around in the great hall like a dervish. You woke the following day in your bed. Even now, you still can't remember how you were able to get home without being picked up by the cops and dropped off in A&E at Sainte-Anne Hospital.

You hadn't stopped sending me emails, and it was my job to forward them on to the court of heaven so they'd take pity on me. You mistook the highways and byways of the internet for the ways of God, as baffling to saints and the faithful as they are to infidels like you. When, some months after my passing, my parents chanced upon them as they sifted through my computer, they probably wished they could give me a ring and advise me to stop going out with such a lunatic.

You wept so much for me that I felt ashamed on your behalf. I could see you through my wooden coffin as you entered the church, like the comic turn in a melodrama, sobbing away disgustingly, all hiccupping and red in the face like someone with whooping cough. You could have put on a balaclava, dark glasses or a Mickey Mouse mask, or even just stayed at home snivelling under the shower so as not to make a mess. The dead don't quench their thirst with the eyes of the living, so they'd better save the juice in their tear ducts for salting the roads!

What a massive favour I've done you, leaving before the carnival's over! For the first time in your life it seemed like your cynicism was sinking under the weight of a concrete sarcophagus! You felt you'd reached the pinnacle of glory! You were carrying death on your shoulders, as if you'd become Christ's half-brother! The bastard offspring God might have had in His old age with a professional mourner! Poor little man, pouring with tears! You're still a megalomaniac, even with your heart broken!

Couldn't you have kept your grief to yourself? A treasure chest crammed with misery, spilling over with the doubloons of despair – but a treasure chest all the same. You've frittered them all away! You wanted to see them tracing a glittering arc from Paris to Jerusalem, all those prayers like flaming torches, lighting up roads and seas, streets and villages, even megacities! You wanted everyone to taste your sorrow! Licking their lips, chewing it, savouring it, before piously spitting it out again in the first place of worship they came across!

"You pervert! You've made an exhibition of myself!"

Grief isn't like fire, tears can't put it out. You could have wept for me without them running down your cheeks; there are those who never sweat in the sun. You could have kept quiet; some people don't breathe a word even under torture, and can barely be heard screaming.

You weren't able to stop your brain churning out words, but you could have been wary of writing them down. You've still got time to erase them, to delete all those letters. But you won't be so considerate. You'll throw me to the lions, you'll sell me down the river. I'll be turned into a product and have a barcode stuck on my back. I'll finish up like a banknote, or a coin. In short, I'll be tagged with a price.

"I'll make you a profit, my little pimp!"

You wouldn't be the first: Hugo made money from his daughter. Léopoldine was drowned, Charlotte hanged herself. She wound up in a poem, and I'm ending up in a novel. She made it into the history books, and thanks to your intervention I might have the lesser distinction of making it onto television. Because you'll clearly have to explain your actions and make a full confession. You'll probably claim I'm a work of fiction, a woman who sprang fully-dressed from your imagination. People will pretend to believe you, as they're polite and far too busy to give a damn. You might at least stop crying, and prove yourself worthy of a Charlotte who was anything but a softy.

I'm sending you a kiss. Roles can be reversed, after all, and this time let Judas be the one to get a peck on the cheek. Apart from me, who'd begrudge you for being a traitor? Love stories can be so very dull without a whiff of death or betrayal.

Dear Charlotte,

I did what I could. I chose to write because I'm no composer. A concerto would have been less vulgar, and much more elegant. A requiem would have been fitting, with mysterious words scribed by some unknown hand and drawn from the golden years of the Middle Ages. If I'd had even an ounce of faith – or been enough of a coward to seek refuge in the supernatural through fear of bad times to come – I'd have grovelled on all fours, just in case. Writing you a story was my way of trying to overcome death. You know very well I didn't succeed.

It's now the end of December, the 23rd in fact, and this time last year you were leaving for Amsterdam. I'm closing this book like a surgeon resigned to stitching up the incision he's made in a young woman's corpse, after a somewhat fanciful operation aimed at bringing her back to life. Writers are so big-headed that even the impossible seems within reach. They're stubborn and dishonest, and want to crow about their most crushing defeats as though they were glorious victories.

So let me ask one last favour of you. Pretend to reply once again. Grant me the satisfaction of one final tantrum.

Allow me to be obnoxious one last time.

"Tell me I had every reason to write this novel."

A ludicrous request, I know. But a writer must put up with lapsing into ridicule, because otherwise he wouldn't even be human.

My poor darling,

I'm less human than you: humanity is no more than a passing phase. You'd like me to give you one last sign of my love, but perhaps someone who hasn't loved to the point of ridicule has never really loved at all. Had I known when I was alive that you'd desert me in the gloom of a novel as grim as this, I haven't the faintest idea – now that I'm dead – what on earth I might have thought.

I've had enough of the rhyming stuff. I'm going now. I'm heading off. You've made me talk a lot; never has a dead woman babbled so much. We chat all night and split up as dawn breaks, because without our bodies we'll never make love. One may lie, and fantasise, but flesh and bone can't be invented on the spot. It's better to be alone than in bad company, and we parted company so long ago. We're separated by nothingness until the day you're part of it as well.

You've turned me into just what you always wanted. You think of books as a womb and me as its baby, saved from drowning. Poor little child: now you can see that your writing has given birth to a skeleton. I had one already, so you could have saved yourself the trouble.

I can hear you saying that skeletons survive intact for thousands of years. From their bones, one can deduce what these creatures were like, conjure them up, reveal them to all. And when those remains belong to humans, even their faces burst into life, grinning back at us from the Stone Age. So I'll forgive you for turning me into words and syllables. Just think: there's every chance a reader might, on occasion, catch a glimpse of me smiling too. What I said to you once, I shall say yet again.

"I'm proud of you."